Death at the Fireside Inn

A 1920s Historical Mystery - book 1

Kitty Kildare

K.E. O'Connor Books

Chapter 1

It wasn't every day I found myself on my hands and knees, peering under a chair, trying to coax a terrified animal out of the corner it had hidden itself in. At the most, it happened once a week.

"I know you're scared, but you don't want Hetty to come after you with that dreadful broom again, do you?" I whispered.

The cowering, smooth-coated black pug had his back to me, curled into a tiny ball, his tail tucked between his legs.

"You've got the courage to come out from under there. And when you do, I've got sausage for you." I extracted a small piece of sausage from the paper bag tucked in its usual place in my warm wool velour hunter green overcoat, and held it out as far as I could for the pug. His body stopped quivering for a second. "That's it! I've not yet met a dog who can resist sausage from our local butcher. Mr Parsons provides high-quality products."

I was in the butcher's so often buying delicacies for the animals I looked after that Mr Parsons had taken to calling me 'Sausage' as a term of endearment. And since he knew where most of that delicious sausage ended up, he was kind enough to give me a hefty discount.

"Miss Vale! If you don't mind me saying, you'll ruin your skirt if you stay down there much longer." Hetty Bishop appeared in the doorway of the sitting room, a large stiff brush in her hand and a scowl on her lined face. "Use this to move it."

I waved away the offer of the unwelcome broom. "Peregrine needs time to understand he's under no threat. And he's grieving, so he's particularly sensitive."

She harrumphed her disbelief. "Animals don't grieve. All they care about is who will give them their next meal."

I left a piece of sausage under the wingback floral patterned chair and sat back on my heels, fixing her with a stern look. "And when did he get his last meal?"

She sniffed. "I'm here to clean, not to look after the animals. And that one needs to go. It made a mess in the back parlour. The rug is beyond saving."

"Most likely because his usual routine has been upended."

"As has mine. I'm out of a job!" Hetty flicked the broom at a speck of dust. "I've only stayed on because I'm paid up to the end of the week. And I want things to look nice. Flo may be gone, but she was good to me. A salt of the earth, despite her lofty career."

"I'm sure she was. And I'm sure she'll appreciate you keeping things tidy for her." Although from the cobwebs under this chair, Hetty wasn't thorough with her cleaning.

"I need to tidy in here. I've already stayed late and can't be wasting no more time on you and that animal."

"This animal is terrified and hungry. He'll get all the time he deserves."

"Let me give it another thump with my broom. That will get it moving."

I stood slowly, set my hands on my hips, and glowered at the woman until she looked away. "The way we treat animals is a testament to our own character."

Hetty turned and stalked along the hallway towards the kitchen. "Ten more minutes, and then you're both out. I'll call the police if I have to."

I intended to go after her, but a small woof from Peregrine made me pause. There was no point in giving the cleaner a piece of my mind. I wasn't here for her. This grieving pug had recently lost his owner, so I had hastened over here as soon as possible, getting the scantest details as to the events that led to the pug owner's death.

So, I was somewhat surprised when I found myself in Mayfair, London. The houses were large, and the incomes equally so. The cleaner, Hetty, hadn't been best pleased to let me in, but my contact, an acquaintance living in Epsom, had telephoned earlier that day to let Hetty know I'd be visiting to collect the pug.

Unfortunately, Peregrine was terrified, and according to Hetty, the poor creature had been hiding in various dark corners in the house ever since his owner died.

I stepped into the hallway, my gaze sweeping the faded grandeur surrounding me, and I took a moment to admire the elegant décor. It was dated but hinted at an availability of money. I cocked an ear as Hetty's harsh tones drifted towards me. She was describing me as a stuck-up busybody who should mind her own business.

I cared nothing about what she thought of me. My concern was rescuing this animal, and I knew exactly where to take him.

I walked confidently back into the sitting room. I peeked under the chair and was pleased to see the sausage I'd left had vanished. That was progress. As soon as the dog trusted me, I'd be able to catch him. Pugs were stubborn little creatures, but once you won them over, you had a loyal, cheeky friend for life.

Perching carefully on the edge of the chair Peregrine had hidden himself behind, I placed another sliver of sausage in my hand and tucked my fingers under the seat. I was prepared to wait it out, even if Hetty wasn't. There was no point in grabbing the animal or scaring it into surrender. That only created a terrified creature. And terrified creatures usually bit!

While I waited for Peregrine to make his move, I inspected the photographs on the wall. All famous theatre stars from the turn of the century. I wasn't a theatre buff, but I recognised most of them. Many of those faces had done sterling work during the Great War, involving themselves in tours to rally the troops, being a part of morale-boosting films that improved soldier and public morale, and generally providing an incredible service when times were at their bleakest.

A small, soft nose nuzzled my fingers as the sausage was taken.

"Good boy. If you come out, you can have as much sausage as you like," I whispered.

We repeated the routine several times: sausage on fingers, Peregrine taking his time, then finally being brave enough to eat.

After the fourth piece of sausage had been taken, I slid back onto my knees and peered under the chair. Peregrine looked back at me with large shining chocolate-coloured eyes, blinked once, and whimpered. He had an adorable, squashed-looking face. Around his neck was a large, sparkly collar.

I set a small row of sausage pieces on the floor, each one closer to me, and I waited.

Peregrine waited too. Stubborn pup.

Eventually, the sausage line won, and he wriggled out on his belly to gobble each piece down, creeping closer to me with each bite. When he got to the last piece of sausage, he wolfed it down, looked up at me, and gave a gentle bark.

"We're friends now, I see. Excellent news. You come with me. No more of this hiding nonsense," I said.

The pug tensed when I went to pick him up, but within a few seconds of being in my arms, he remembered how good it felt to be snuggled, because he relaxed.

"At last!" Hetty reappeared at the door, and Peregrine growled at her. "You caught the nuisance. His brother and him were such pests whenever I worked. They were always getting in the way or nipping at my ankles."

"There's another pug in residence?" I asked. "I was only told about one in need of collection."

Hetty waved a hand in the air. "It's not here! I put together a box of the animal's things. If you don't take them, I'll only throw them out."

"I'll take the toys. Peregrine will welcome his familiar things since his world has been so grievously upturned."

"It's by the front door." Hetty shook her head as she regarded the pug with a shrewish look. "Florence treated those creatures like they were babies, not animals."

"It's a point of fact that we are all animals," I said.

Hetty sniffed again. "Not by my reckoning. Time for you to go. You got what you came for."

I stopped by a photograph hanging from a picture rail on the wall. "Your former employer must have been someone of note. These pictures are of famous people."

Hetty looked at me as if I'd said something ridiculous. "Of course she was. Everyone knew Flo. And they all loved her. Mind you, they wouldn't have been so fond of her if they had to clean up after her. She was almost as messy as her dogs, God rest her soul."

"Florence was in the theatre business?"

"She was. You really must leave. I have so much to do." Hetty marched to the door, lifted a box, and held it out to me.

I followed her to the door. "What about the other dog? I may as well collect them both. Where will I find him?"

Hetty tilted her head. "You don't know what happened to Flo?"

"All I was told was there was an animal that needed rescuing because his owner died. I knew the woman's name was Florence, and I was given this address. Is there something else I should know?"

Hetty pulled herself upright. "I should have said earlier. They found the other dog with Flo's body. It'll most likely be in the pound or have run off if the coppers didn't grab it. That one was always escaping out the door if you didn't watch for it."

This news didn't thrill me. The police dog pound was a notoriously unpleasant place, all cold floors and metal, and whenever I could, I got the dogs out and arranged for them to be fostered, or moved them to the much more appealing dogs' home on the other side of the river.

"Where did Florence die?" I asked.

Hetty looked smug at having more information than I did, but I tried not to let it bristle.

"I don't like to gossip," she finally said.

"I'm sure you'll make an exception on this occasion. Once I know everything, I'll take this pug, and you'll never see either of us again."

"Florence took the dogs with her when she worked," Hetty said. "But that one you're holding wasn't feeling well, so she left it behind. She was supposed to be home that night, but she never showed."

"Did that not concern you?"

"I don't live in. I have lodgings across town, so I didn't know she hadn't come home. Flo has several London homes, or she'd stay at a nearby hotel when she was working."

"She died in a hotel?"

"I can't tell you where she died. When the police came here, they said she'd passed last night after her performance. She was found when her other dog, Quillon, alerted to a problem. It kept barking." Hetty's expression grew sharp and shrivelled, as if she smelled something unpleasant. "The coppers wouldn't tell me anything else, despite having worked for Flo for thirty years. If you need to know more, go to the Winter Garden Theatre. That was her second home, and where she held her last performance. The staff there should know more."

I drew in a sharp breath. My gaze went to the sitting room with its photographs of dazzling bygone era theatre stars. "Flo. Florence. Are you talking about the theatre star, Florence Sterling?"

"And now the penny drops. The very same. And you're standing in her home, holding one of her pugs," Hetty said. "Aren't you the lucky one?"

Chapter 2

It had just passed seven o'clock in the evening as I hailed a taxi outside of Florence Sterling's house and climbed in with Peregrine securely tucked under my arm.

"Where to, miss?" the cabbie asked.

"The dogs' home on Battersea Park Road. Please hurry." I'd have preferred to walk, but this was an emergency, and it would have taken almost an hour on foot.

I glanced down at Peregrine, his belly full and his body no longer quivering, and gently stroked him. I had to admit to being shocked by Hetty's news. Florence Sterling was dead! I'd seen her perform several times, and she was a darling of the theatre world.

Not only was I shocked to learn of the death of such a popular performer, but I'd met Florence several times. It felt like an acquaintance had died.

So great was my shock, I barely noticed the bustling streets of London as the taxi made its way through the traffic and travelled past groups heading off to enjoy their evening's entertainment. Ever since the war had ended, people were making the most of their freedom, and I'd heard many say you never knew what was around the corner, so they were living in the moment. From all the fur and fripperies on display, despite the inclement weather, I could well believe they all carried that motto in their hearts.

We reached our destination, and I paid the taxi driver and climbed out. I struggled to balance the box of toys on my hip and the snoozing dog on the other, so I was delighted to see my best friend, Ruby Smythe, waiting for me, just as she promised she would be when I had telephoned from a public phone box before hailing the taxi.

"Who do we have here?" Ruby smiled indulgently at the small dog who snuggled against me for warmth. Her dark hair was hidden under a fashionable cloche hat, and she wore a matching navy woollen coat.

"This is Peregrine," I said. "We're here to hunt for his brother. I'm hoping the police have done the right thing and brought him here."

"I'll take that." Ruby took the heavy box of dog toys I'd brought with me. "Gosh! There are more toys in here than most children see in their entire lives."

"There's an excellent reason for that." I hurried with her towards the entrance to the dogs' home. "These pugs belonged to Florence Sterling."

Ruby's eyes widened. "I've seen her perform! She was beautiful. Her skin always looked flawless, despite her advancing years. Although, I've not heard much about her since the end of the war. She did sterling work to gee up the chaps in the trenches. Florence had a connection to your family, didn't she?"

"She did. She'd take a room at the Fireside Inn before she performed at the Winter Garden Theatre. That was before the war," I said. "I wonder if she rented her old room while she was performing."

"It wouldn't surprise me if she did. Famous types can be superstitious. Never say the name of the Scottish play before a performance. Always wear the same undergarments. Turn around three times and curtsy before you step onto the stage." Ruby laughed. "I remember your father was fond of Florence."

I smiled. "When she stayed at the inn, he would tease her about rubbing shoulders with the riffraff. But she came up from nothing, and used her magnificent figure and beautiful face to get where she wanted. Florence once said to my father she'd never forget where she came from."

Ruby chuckled. "Your old dad would flirt with anyone, from servant to staff. And he could never resist a pretty face."

My father, Davey Vale, came from the same working-class background as Florence. He'd worked his way up from nothing, buying rundown pubs and taverns across Britain and Ireland and turning them into prosperous businesses. Depending on which rumours you listened to, the way he went about business wasn't always legitimate, but he left my elderly mother, me, and my younger brother, Matthew, well provided for. And whenever we needed to stay somewhere, there was always a room available in one of the many establishments that had our name above the door.

We hurried out of the cold to find Molly Banbury settled in her usual seat behind the reception desk. The dogs' home was a large building, kept meticulously clean, as the scent of bleach tickling my nose testified.

There was the usual bustle of activity as volunteers dashed around, working with the dogs to get them fed and walked. It was a never-ending cycle, wrapped up in a bundle of fur, wagging tails, and barking.

"Veronica! What a treat. And Ruby! I've got just the thing for you. Or should I say, just the four-legged friend. Well, three legs, but who's counting?" Molly stood from her seat. She was a robust fifty with tight ginger curls. The eyepatch she wore partly contained those robust curls. Molly had almost lost her life when her neighbour's house had been struck by a German bomb in Wandsworth. She wore her scars bravely, although they sometimes troubled her.

"I'm still not on the market," Ruby said sternly, a smile playing about her lips.

"This one is perfect for you. A match made in heaven."

They played this game every time they met, Molly trying to get Ruby to adopt a dog, and Ruby pretending she didn't have room or time for an animal.

"Wait until you see his adorable face," Molly said. "This one's a heartbreaker."

"No! I refuse to fall in love with anything with fur. Now, if you have something with hooves I could ride, we could do business."

"I've got a new one for you," I said to Molly. "I just picked him up. Peregrine's owner died. I believe you have his brother."

Molly ducked and inspected the pug. "We don't get many of that breed in here. I'm sure I'd have remembered if we took in an adorable face like that. Give me a moment to check the records. Any idea when he arrived?" She was already thumbing through a long list of intakes. The dogs' home needed to be twice the size it was to care for the abandoned animals around London, but we did the best we could with the resources we had, no matter how thinly they were spread.

"It must have been within the last twenty-four hours," I said.

Molly kept her attention on the list as she ran a finger down it. "Where's Benji?"

"At home with my mother. She wasn't feeling well, so Benji wanted to keep her company, curled up asleep at the bottom of her bed." My beloved rescue dog loved his sleep as much as he loved long brisk walks.

"I'm sure that was the real reason." Molly looked out at the freezing grey evening, her expression wry. "If I could use that as an excuse to stay home, curled up under my covers, I would."

"Same here," Ruby said. "All this grey gets me down."

"Still waiting for your handsome action hero to sweep you away to a Tuscan paradise?" Molly chortled to herself.

Ruby blushed. "If I desire such an adventure, I'll jolly well take myself on one."

Molly smiled warmly at her. "We had a beautiful long-haired Saluki brought in recently. He was a terrified, matted creature, but with a bit of love, he could be a show dog. Are you sure I can't tempt you? Much better than a pesky hero."

Ruby resolutely shook her head. "You know I'm more of a horsewoman."

"He has the sweetest face," Molly said. "You could teach him to canter, just like a horse. He has long legs. All three of them!"

"I'm happy to be auntie to Benji, volunteer here when I'm able, and ride all the horses I can in my spare time," Ruby said. "That's enough responsibility for me."

After the war, Ruby had taken a job as a private secretary to a wealthy, retired widow who was horse obsessed. Combine that with Ruby's work in equine supply logistics during the war, and they were a horse-mad match made in heaven. I wasn't sure how much work they actually did, unless you counted riding horses and visiting stables to see what new horses could be acquired, work, but Ruby was blissfully happy.

"No pugs brought in," Molly said. "No drop-offs from the police in the last few days. It's a surprise. They usually bring a few in."

I pressed my lips together. I'd worked hard with the local police to get them to bring unwanted or lost animals here. The dogs' home was a welcoming, comforting space for animals. It was so much better than the sterile police pound.

Ruby touched my elbow, knowing what I was thinking. "We'll get him out of the pound."

"We will. And I see refresher training for the police is in order," I grumbled. "If no one is looking after him, he could have escaped from the theatre and ended up on the streets. Pampered creatures like that pug are vulnerable. He's used to high tea and silken cushions, not the rush of a car zooming by and busy streets."

"I'm sure your friend Inspector Templeton will help us track him down," Ruby said with a sly smile. "It's been at least a month since you've argued with him. That makes you practically best friends."

Inspector Jacob Templeton was a thorn in my side, although he could occasionally be a helpful thorn. He'd been the officer who had allowed me to get a foot in the door to provide unofficial training to the Metropolitan Police to ensure they knew there was a refuge for abandoned animals. Still, I would hardly call him a friend. I'll never forget the occasion he called me 'wilful' and 'interfering.' But it was better to deal with the devil you knew.

"We'll try at the Winter Garden Theatre first," I said. "Perhaps the police kept the dog there. Florence took the pugs to her shows, so the staff could be familiar with him."

"I'll let you know if he's brought in," Molly said.

"Have you got space for this one?" I attempted to pry Peregrine off my hip, but he whimpered and rested his head on my chest, melting my heart with his big brown eyes.

Molly bit her lip and glanced over her shoulder. "We're bursting at the seams. The council did a sweep of the slums a month ago, brought in all those strays. Do you remember?"

I softly sighed. The council had wanted to clean the streets before Christmas, and as a result, many strays living in the abandoned, bomb-damaged buildings had been removed, along with more than a handful of homeless people. The dogs' home had rallied and opened their doors to as many animals as they could handle. It was still not enough.Top of Form

"Not even a small pen? I'm sure I can find Peregrine a new home quickly. His owner was well connected, so one of Florence's friends may have room for him.

Someone will want him." I just needed to find the right someone who had room in their heart for two grieving angels who wanted love and a cozy bed.

"He looks settled with you," Molly said. "He could become Benji's new best friend."

"Not another foster!" Ruby said. "Veronica, you've only just re-homed all those cats. And Matthew is looking after kittens, isn't he?"

"Benji always enjoys having a new companion," Molly said. "He can take care of the pug while you work."

I gently stroked the dog's head. "I suppose he is only small. He can keep Mother company while I'm at the paper."

"That's the spirit," Molly said. "If only we had a few thousand more like you, we'd have no problems with abandoned animals on the streets."

"Is there anyone who can give him a quick check?" I asked. "Providing he's healthy, I'll take him."

"Give me twenty minutes. We've still got two volunteer vets on duty. One of them will look him over." Molly took the reluctant pug from me and bustled away.

"Once Peregrine is settled, it's time to give the police a piece of my mind," I said.

Ruby grinned, no doubt recognising the gleam of anger in my eyes. "I shall reserve a front-row seat for that performance."

"You're welcome to attend. And after we've done that, we will find out exactly what happened to Florence Sterling at the Winter Garden Theatre and where her missing pug is."

Chapter 3

The taxi dropped us outside my family home, close to Seven Sisters Road in Finsbury Park. Since I had Peregrine with me, it seemed unfair to stride around London with him on my hip. The poor creature was confused enough, without a brisk walk on a cold night, adding to his worries.

I paid the cabbie, and we hurried in, out of the damp evening. The chill of winter still had its hold on the city, and spring seemed a long way away.

Benji, my ever faithful four-legged companion, was sitting by the front door as if he knew I was due back at that time. His attention went to the pug, and his tan-furred head cocked.

"We have a new temporary addition to the family," I said. "You need to be kind to him. Peregrine's just lost his owner."

Benji was a friend to all animals, and always welcomed them into our fur-covered home. He was a rescue animal himself, although I often thought we'd rescued each other during a terribly dark moment in our lives. He knew when to stay calm around new arrivals and give them space so they could adjust to the strange situation they found themselves in. He was also an excellent playmate and drew out the most timid of animals when they were ready.

"Veronica, is that you?" My mother's tremulous voice drifted from the vast downstairs room she had taken over as her main bedroom.

"It's me," I said. "I brought Ruby with me, and someone to keep you company when I'm working."

"Don't let them stand on ceremony in the hallway. Bring them in. I've been on my own all day."

I exchanged a wry smile with Ruby. My mother, Edith Vale, lived with me and my brother, Matthew. We also had wonderful neighbours who dropped in most days for a gossip and a cup of tea, and there were always furry or feathered refugees as residents, who kept my mother company. She was rarely alone, although her grouchy grumbling suggested otherwise.

Matthew appeared from the kitchen, holding a cup in one hand, an affable smile on his face as he scratched his fingers through his pale, messy hair. Hair that looked like it hadn't been brushed for days. He wore a misbuttoned pale blue shirt and pyjama bottoms. He blushed when he saw Ruby, although she'd seen him much scruffier.

"What have you got there?" he said by way of greeting.

"Mrs Florence Sterling's dog," I said. "Meet Peregrine."

"Hi, Peregrine. Who's Florence Sterling?"

"Matthew Vale!" Ruby scolded. "She was one of the biggest stars of the theatre, and you must have seen her morale-boosting films when you served."

His expression blanked for a second. "Can't say I remember any films. The kettle has boiled if you want a brew. We're low on tea leaves, though." He ambled away and headed up the stairs, back to the mess of a bedroom he rarely came out of unless there was food on offer.

"I'll go in and say hello to your mother," Ruby said.

That left me with the task of introducing Benji to the pug. It went smoothly, and the dogs were soon sniffing noses and other parts, so I felt comfortable to leave Peregrine on the floor. The pug even wagged his little stubby tail when Benji offered him his favourite green ball to play with. Benji always shared his toys.

I hurried into the kitchen, brewed the tea, keeping an eye on the dogs, then walked into my mother's bedroom with a full tea tray in my hands. Mother's room was a welcoming muddle of interest. There were trinkets from her travels with my father, stacks of well-thumbed books, and dark, oversized Victorian era furniture, including a huge wrought iron bed with a pile of pillows and cushions and plenty of blankets. The air always smelled faintly of talcum powder and rose water.

My mother was sixty-one, with grey-white hair and lines around her mouth that made her look like she was frowning. Despite the stern exterior, she had a soft heart and a love of animals almost as big as mine. Ever since my father died, she'd complained of various ailments and ill health, regularly taking to her bed for several weeks to recover. I often thought it wasn't so much an illness but a broken heart she suffered from. My father had been no saint, but they'd adored each other until the end.

"You're back late! I was worried something terrible had happened to you." My mother took the tea I'd made her, and I handed another cup to Ruby.

"Something bad has happened, although not to me," I said. "I can't stay for long, but I wanted to check on you. Are you well?"

"You must not go out again. You'll catch a chill. Or influenza. I heard from Gladys that cases of pneumonia are on the rise, so wear a warm scarf tomorrow. Or better yet, stay at home. I have the doctor visiting. He can examine you, too. Your complexion worries me."

"My complexion is as it should be for someone who has been out in this weather. The doctor doesn't need to see me. What is he visiting you for?"

"The usual. Heart spasms. And I can't sleep."

"A nip of brandy should see you right," Ruby said.

"No brandy! Not with your medication," I said.

Mother sipped her tea, not looking happy. "Where is the other person you brought to visit me?"

"Lean over the edge of your bed and you'll see him," I said. "He's making friends with Benji."

She tutted at me, although there was a gleam of happiness in her eyes. "Another stray! Veronica, we don't have the room."

"We have more rooms than we need."

"This one isn't a mysterious stray. Peregrine was a seriously pampered pug." Ruby was rifling through the box of toys she'd brought in from the taxi. "I was just telling your mother about Florence Sterling's death."

Mother nodded sagely. "Terrible business. Poor woman. Still, she was around the same age as me. It could happen to us at any time. My heart's been fluttering all day. I never know when it'll give out."

"You're as healthy as a purebred fox terrier. And as feisty as one." I briefly checked her temperature and pulse. She was comfortably warm and had a steady heartbeat.

"Old age can grab you at any time," my mother said. "Put him on the bed, then. Let's see what I'm dealing with. I hope he's well behaved."

I dutifully collected Peregrine, who was tussling with Benji, and introduced him to my mother. After a few seconds of nervousness, he realised she was a pushover as she produced a packet of Brown's dog treats from her bedside cabinet and offered him one.

"There's another pug, too," I said. "Apparently, Florence took them everywhere with her. This one wasn't well, so she left him at home when she went to perform."

"We're off to get the other one," Ruby said. "And see what we can find out about what happened to Florence."

"Most likely a heart attack." Mother gently patted the pug. "All that stress of being in the limelight. And the way she carried on with the men. No wonder her heart gave up!"

"We don't know if it was a heart attack. Grab a dog blanket from the box," I said to Ruby. "Peregrine's brother will be more comfortable if he has something familiar to smell. And I'll take Benji, too."

"Can't you go tomorrow?" my mother asked. "It's getting late, and you have work in the morning."

"We'll be back within the hour," I said. "You don't want an innocent, sad little pup left on his own after what happened to his owner, do you?"

She swatted me lightly with a pale, veined hand. "Of course not. But no walking the streets late at night. There are all kinds of rough types out there."

"I shall insist we take a taxi," Ruby said. "My heels aren't meant for stomping around the streets."

"Very sensible," my mother said. "I'll watch this little fellow. Make sure he settles in."

I kissed my mother's cheek, and after several minutes of her warning me about the dangers of the London streets, gangs, the cads, and the risk of contracting a grievous illness due to the cold, I was outside with Ruby and Benji, and we swiftly found a taxi to take us to the Winter Garden Theatre.

As the driver pulled up, it was clear to see all was not well. Police officers stood outside guarding the main entrance, adding two unwelcome pillars to the otherwise impressive building, with its clock tower frontage and giant billboards announcing the latest shows for people to enjoy.

"I don't recognise either of them," Ruby said. "We may not get an easy pass into the theatre."

"We're here on a matter of important business," I said. "They'll have to let us in."

Ruby didn't seem convinced, but I strode to the police officers with Benji by my side. "Good evening. I'm here to pick up a dog."

The younger of the two officers, no more than twenty-five with unruly black eyebrows, barely spared me a glance. "Sorry, Miss. No one is allowed in. There's been an incident."

"I know. Florence Sterling is dead. I'm here to collect her pug."

He flashed me a startled look before regaining his composure. "I can't help you there."

"There was a small pug inside, though? About this big." I extended my hands to demonstrate the dimensions of said pug. "Possibly black fur if he's a match for his brother. Goes by the name Quillon."

"Move along, Miss."

I turned my attention to the other officer, whose gaze was fixed ahead and his hands behind his back. "I'll be five minutes. I'll touch nothing. I just need to find the dog. He should have been taken directly to the dogs' home in Battersea. Do you know the place?"

"You'll have to come back when the theatre is open to the public," he said.

"I'm going nowhere until I've checked to see if there's a terrified animal inside." I arched an eyebrow when neither officer stepped aside. "Perhaps I could speak to your superior. Is Inspector Templeton leading this case?"

There was a brief flash of surprise on both the officers' faces.

"If he's here, that means foul play is involved," I said to Ruby. Inspector Jacob Templeton was the lead detective in most local murders.

"You can contact Inspector Templeton in the morning," the younger officer said. "Don't make a nuisance of yourself."

"We're hardly doing that. We're concerned members of the public looking to offer our assistance," Ruby said. "I say, you look jolly good in that uniform. How long have you been on the job?"

While Ruby attempted to flirt with the officers, I discreetly stepped back and gestured at Benji to run. We regularly trained together, and he'd been quick to pick up spoken and visual commands, so it was a simple task to instruct him to dart past the officers.

"Oh! I'm so sorry. My dog is badly behaved. I must grab him in case he bites someone." I dodged past the officers before they could argue. "Ruby, I need your help. Benji is such a handful. We won't be a moment. So sorry, again."

Ruby's heels tapped along behind me as we hurried around the side of the Winter Garden Theatre, ignoring the protests from the officers. We had no time to spare, although I was confident, they wouldn't abandon their posts to chase two fickle females and their hound. More fool them.

There were always side entrances at theatres where performers could slip out when they needed to avoid the crowds, so I was convinced we'd find one. Luckily for us, a door was unlocked, and we swiftly slipped inside, Benji with us, having waited like a good boy. We'd only taken ten steps along the gloomy corridor when the lights came on overhead.

Inspector Jacob Templeton stood at the end of the corridor, dressed in his uniform, a scowl on his face.

"Oh! You startled me. What a surprise to see you here," I said.

"Is it?" He strode towards us. He was six-foot two inches with dark hair and intense dark eyes. Some may call him handsome. I considered him mostly rude. "I just had one of my officers report on two women attempting to break into the theatre. My thoughts immediately turned to Veronica Vale and her faithful sidekick. And what a surprise, here you are."

"I'm not a sidekick!" Ruby exclaimed. "I'm a leading lady."

"I meant Benji."

Ruby set her hands on her hips. "We made it perfectly clear what our intentions were. We're not snooping. We're on a vital rescue mission."

I nodded. "Quite right. We're here for the dog. I told your officers that, but they wouldn't listen to sense. They wouldn't even answer my questions to let me know if Florence's dog was here."

Inspector Templeton held out his hand as Benji sniffed around him and then scratched behind his furry ears. "The dog is here. Quillon is safe. I would have called you tomorrow about him when I had more time. How did you know he was at the theatre?"

"Lucky guess. Although I collected his brother, Peregrine, from Florence's Mayfair home this evening," I said. "I'm looking after him until we can find him a proper home."

"And you couldn't resist poking around to find out what happened to Florence, I suppose?" Inspector Templeton stood up from petting Benji.

"Naturally, I'm curious. Florence Sterling was a big name in the theatre. And I'm even more interested now you're involved in the case. You being here suggests this is a crime scene."

"If it is, you're not to touch anything," Inspector Templeton said. "Nor you, Ruby."

"We promise we'll barely breathe on anything," I said. "Although you may need to bribe Benji with treats, so he behaves. He enjoys sticking his nose in places he shouldn't."

As if to demonstrate, Benji poked his nose into Inspector Templeton's crotch, making him jump back and gently shoo him away.

"The officer said your out-of-control dog ran off." Inspector Templeton shook his head. "I know Benji. You made him do that, so you could sneak inside."

"As if I have control over such a free-spirited animal." I repressed a gentle smirk. "Take me to the pug. He is my priority."

Inspector Templeton sighed. "This way."

We walked along the recently whitewashed corridor, up a set of steps, and into the main lobby of the theatre, decorated in a French style, with posters displaying recent musical comedy numbers and plays, including Kissing Time by Guy Bolton and P.G. Woodhouse.

Inspector Templeton's pace was brisk, but I was happy to match it. "I don't like to appear pushy, Inspector Templeton—"

"You always do, so why change the habit of a lifetime?" he said.

I exchanged an exasperated glance with Ruby. "Unless your role in the Metropolitan Police has changed, you're here because Florence's death wasn't from natural causes. Is that correct?"

"Perhaps I've been given a promotion. Moved to the fraud cases."

"Have you? Are congratulations in order?"

He kept walking, and we kept following, out of the main lobby, into the theatre, down the steps, and past the seats.

"I had a passing acquaintance with Florence," I said. "If I may be so bold, that connection could be helpful to your investigation."

Inspector Templeton stopped walking and turned to me. "You knew the victim?"

"Victim! So, Florence was murdered!" Ruby's eyes widened. "What happened to her?"

Inspector Templeton squeezed the bridge of his nose. "There is evidence to suggest foul play. How did you know Florence?"

"Not well, but she stayed at the Fireside Inn when she performed here," I said. "My father knew her better than I did. I was young when she was in her heyday, but we met several times. She once let me wear her brightest red lipstick. My mother was horrified."

He nodded slowly. "Interesting. Florence performed here the night she died. The Fireside Inn isn't far from this location, so she could have taken her old room."

"Perhaps she did," I said. "Why don't you show me yours, and I'll show you mine."

It was a calculated risk, but as Ruby had rightly pointed out, theatre types were a superstitious lot and kept to the same routine to ensure good luck during performances. If my memory served me, Florence liked staying in the same room at the Fireside Inn, so I was confident she'd have done the same during this tour.

A muscle in Inspector Templeton's jaw twitched. He nodded. "I can confirm it's a crime scene."

"The grim-faced coppers on the door rather gave that away," Ruby said.

"May we view said scene?" I gently pressed. "I could see something out of sorts."

"You'll definitely see that. Florence's body is still here." Inspector Templeton narrowed his gaze. "This is no place for civilians."

"I'm an observant woman." I inched closer and lowered my gaze in an effort to be demure. "Inspector, you know me. We can be helpful to each other. I can be useful to you."

"Just here for the dog, are you?" Inspector Templeton muttered something under his breath. "You can look, but you must stay by the door. And don't faint. It's not a pretty scene."

A thrill of pensive excitement shimmered through me. I was used to unpretty and downright ugly. "If you would be so kind as to show us the way, let's see what we're dealing with."

Chapter 4

A swell of sadness churned through my stomach as I stood with Ruby and Benji by the open door of the dressing room. Florence Sterling's name was neatly written on the outside of the door, and inside lay the former theatre darling, slumped at her dressing table. The room had been thoroughly turned over, so whoever had done this had been looking for something of value or something important to them.

Ruby clutched my hand, and Benji softly whined, sensing our distress. There was an officer in the room taking photographs, and another male officer writing things down in a notepad.

"I told you it wasn't pretty," Inspector Templeton said.

"Murder rarely is," I murmured.

"We should have moved her by now, but there's been a delay in getting the vehicle here." His wrinkled brow revealed what he thought of that hold up.

"What's been taken?" I asked.

"Why do you think anything's been taken?"

"Unless Florence did this to her own room, whoever killed her wanted something from here."

Inspector Templeton's nose twitched. "We're questioning the theatre staff to see if anything is missing."

"There's a gap on the awards shelf," Ruby said. "Did someone steal a trophy?"

"We've noted that. Once we've ensured all evidence has been collected, we'll search for the trophy to see if it's relevant to the investigation."

My gaze moved around the room, but kept returning to Florence. It was clear she had a nasty injury to the side of her head. A metal trophy would have been able to inflict that damage.

"What did the theatre staff tell you when you interviewed them?" I asked.

Inspector Templeton shook his head. "That's enough. I'll lose my badge if my boss finds out you've been in here asking questions."

"Nonsense! Detective Chief inspector Taylor adores me. Well, he wants to marry Ruby, so he puts up with me," I said, tipping my friend a wink.

Ruby harrumphed, showing her disbelief at that comment. "He wants to do something extremely unladylike to me, and it doesn't involve putting a ring on my finger. The man is a cad."

"Detective Chief Inspector Taylor is a highly regarded member of the Metropolitan Police." Inspector Templeton shrugged. "But you're right, he's not to be trusted with the ladies."

"Exactly my point! He's asked me on a dozen dates, and each time, I've had to put him in his place. He once had the cheek to suggest we go to a tawdry little guest house in Margate where rooms are rented by the hour," Ruby said.

"He loves to chase the unobtainable." My gaze kept going around the room as I pieced together what had happened during Florence's last moments. "So long as you keep him interested, it gives us some leeway. Although, how did he describe us the last time he caught us snooping into a case?"

"I don't remember." Inspector Templeton looked at his polished black shoes.

"You absolutely do. Refresh our memory. We won't be offended."

Inspector Templeton huffed out a sigh. "He said it would harm your highly strung feminine sensitivities to solve a murder."

"The man is a buffoon!" Ruby said. "Which is perfectly clear, since he chases the flappers and high society girls, rather than settling for a suitable woman who will stop his nonsense."

"He thinks you're a suitable woman," I said. "Maybe that's what he needs, someone who'll put him in his place. Inspector, I was wondering—"

"No! That's enough snooping." Inspector Templeton ushered as into the corridor and into an empty, floral scented dressing room next door to the crime scene.

As annoying as it was to be interrupted and removed from a fascinating, if somewhat gruesome scene, I knew better than to push my luck with the inspector.

"Where's Quillon?" I asked politely. "He wasn't in the dressing room."

"I'll get an officer to bring him in." Inspector Templeton left the room for a few seconds and then returned. "He'll be here shortly. We found the dog with Florence's body. He was reluctant to leave and tried to bite one of my officers."

"That wasn't the dog's fault he attacked," I said. "Quillon would have been terrified. He may even have seen what happened."

"He's a witness to the murder!" Ruby said. "It's a shame you can't question him."

"It would make this investigation simpler to have an eyewitness." Inspector Templeton turned as the door opened, and an officer presented a chunky black smooth-coated pug to him. "Give the dog to Veronica."

The officer handed me the dog. It took several minutes of murmuring to Quillon and gently stroking him before he stopped shaking.

"You'll be fine soon," I whispered. "I'll reunite you with your brother. You have a safe space to sleep and all the food you can dream of. I'm so sorry for your loss."

"According to the theatre manager, Florence always had the dogs with her," Inspector Templeton said.

"So I understand. Do you know what happened to Florence?" I asked. "I saw the head injury, so I assumed that's what killed her."

Inspector Templeton was silent for more than a handful of seconds. I could almost hear his thoughts churning. "I shouldn't disclose information in an ongoing investigation."

I pursed my lips. "I'll most likely write her obituary for the newspaper, so I need to know the details of her death. And given how famous Florence was, it's likely we will do a feature on her. If I don't get the details from you now, someone else will come snooping. Someone pushier."

"Is that even possible?" Inspector Templeton paced the room once, his hands in his pockets. "We believe Florence was killed between midnight and eight o'clock in the morning. Before she died, she performed at the theatre, doing a show of her greatest hits."

"If I'd known, I would have come to the performance," Ruby said. "I enjoy a rousing singsong."

Inspector Templeton continued. "After the performance, Florence had drinks with select guests and VIPs. The party ended around eleven, and everyone left."

"Florence stayed behind on her own?" I asked.

"The theatre manager said that was her routine. She always took time alone in her dressing room, taking off her stage makeup and enjoying a glass of celebratory champagne. When she was ready, she'd leave out of the side entrance. We believe she hailed a taxi."

"Didn't the manager think it strange when Florence didn't leave?" I asked, gently cradling the dog, whose eyes were already half-closed, comfortable in my arms.

"He didn't stay to see what she did. He's worked here for years, and Florence had an arrangement with him. She paid him a little extra to have the place to herself. The manager said she thought of the theatre as her second home, and would wander around drinking her champagne. He trusted her so much, she had her own key."

"Was the side door locked when you arrived?" I asked.

"It was."

"Have you found the key?"

"Not yet."

"The killer could have taken it when they left," I said.

"Why would they do that?"

"I'm thinking aloud. Whoever killed Florence must have known her routine intimately. They knew she'd be alone in the theatre and easy to get to. They could have hidden somewhere after the performance finished and attacked her. Who found Florence?" I asked.

"A member of the cleaning staff. One of the regular women who works here discovered Florence's body. Well, she heard Quillon barking and came to see what was going on. The poor woman fainted when she discovered the scene."

"Did any of the cleaners see anyone else?" I asked. "Maybe the killer was still here when they arrived."

"There are four cleaners who work in the morning to tidy up after the previous night's performance. We have spoken to them. None of them saw or heard anything strange."

"The killer used that missing trophy on Florence," Ruby said with confident assurance. "Find the murder weapon, and that'll help you figure this out."

"Thank you, Miss Smythe. We're looking into all possibilities," Inspector Templeton said. "The one thing we aren't doing is jumping to conclusions. As of this moment, the killer's weapon of choice is unknown."

I gently massaged the pug's head. "There was very little blood."

"There was some blood," Inspector Templeton said.

"Head wounds bleed profusely," I replied. "Even if it's not a serious injury, there is always a shocking amount of blood. People panic when they take a blow to the head because of how much they bleed."

"How do you know that?"

I arched an eyebrow. "We all served, Inspector."

He tilted his head. "You did something on the telephone exchange system during the war, didn't you?"

"To begin with. But I assure you, I expanded my skill set as needs required." My time on active service during the Great War wasn't something I talked about, and much of what I'd done was classified, but I'd seen a fair amount of unpleasant injuries, and that experience had taught me everything I needed to know about head wounds.

"Florence's body will be examined so we can determine the exact cause of death," Inspector Templeton said. "That will provide us with a clearer picture about the murder weapon."

"Not a blade, and unlikely to be a gun," I said. "What about suspects?"

"Veronica! You ask too many questions. This is not your business."

"We're sharing."

"What you're doing is overstepping."

I brushed away his comment with a gentle shrug so as not to disturb Quillon, who was snoring. "Could it have been one of the party guests Florence hosted after her performance? She must have an agent. Perhaps they had a disagreement."

"Or a lover," Ruby said. "Florence's romantic past was torrid. You could write a steamy book about all her adventures with her many men."

"She was married, wasn't she?" I asked.

"Florence has been married at least twice," Ruby said. "There's a current husband. I can't remember his name. A younger man. Very handsome."

"Anyone relevant to this investigation will be questioned by the appropriate people at the appropriate time. You aren't appropriate persons. You got what you came for, so it's time to leave." Inspector Templeton's gaze dropped to the snoozing pug.

"What about an obsessed fan?" I asked. "Famous people often find themselves in trouble when fans cross the boundary from reality into fantasy."

"I agree. There's work to do here," Ruby said.

"Not by either of you," Inspector Templeton said. "You need to leave."

I nodded, although my thoughts were tumbling over each other as I considered the possibilities. "Before I forget, I'd like to arrange more training for the police officers in this area. The dogs' home hasn't been receiving its usual intake of strays. I trust your officers aren't shirking their responsibilities."

"We have other priorities to deal with," Inspector Templeton said, crouching to pet Benji. "But I'll see what I can do. We've had a new intake recently, so they don't know how everything works. There could have been some oversight."

"I'm available whenever you can fit me in. You know the dogs' home is the kindest place for strays."

Inspector Templeton stood to his full height. "Now, I've shown you Florence's dressing room and told you far more than you need to know. Let's see the room Florence stayed at in the Fireside Inn, shall we?"

I gulped down my concern. If Florence had changed her plans and not stayed at the inn, I was about to get into serious trouble for lying to the police.

Chapter 5

"We'll take my car." Inspector Templeton led us through the theatre, into the lobby, and to the main doors.

"The Fireside Inn is a five-minute walk from here," I said. "It's the reason Florence liked staying there. The location was so convenient for her when she finished an evening show."

"It's late, I'm tired, and I won't get home until midnight. The faster we do this, the better. Unless you're hiding something from me."

I slid a glance Ruby's way. "What would we have to hide?"

Inspector Templeton's fixed stare reminded me of the time I startled a sausage-stealing spaniel who refused to rescind his treasure.

"Wait here for me. I'll just be a moment." He walked away and spoke to the two police officers guarding the entrance. One of them glared at me, suggesting my behaviour had caused him embarrassment, but I made no apology for that. Now I knew a crime had been committed against an acquaintance, I was even more determined to ensure this dreadful wrong was corrected.

Inspector Templeton returned with an officer beside him, the young chap with the unruly black eyebrows who had refused us entry. "This is Sergeant Jones."

We greeted each other civilly, then headed outside and climbed into a plain black car parked close by. Ruby, the dogs, and I took the back seat, while Sergeant Jones sat up front with Inspector Templeton. He drove along Drury Lane, onto Longacre, past Covent Garden, and turned onto King Street.

The city of London always held a timeless charm for me, the glow of streetlights revealing fashionable crowds hurrying along the pavements, off to a party, or maybe simply to get home and into the warm. We passed a vibrant jumble of theatres and dance halls, all popular pastimes during and after the war, offering respite in a difficult period of our recent history.

"I've never been to the Fireside Inn," Inspector Templeton said. "What can we expect?"

"It's a quaint place," I said. "It was one of the first pubs my father bought. There are two separate bars and then six rooms upstairs we hire to guests. We usually have visiting tradespeople staying there."

"Does it have a reputation?"

"For excellent ale and service," I said tartly. "All the establishments my family owns are considered decent these days."

"From what I know of the Fireside Inn, sir, it used to be a rough place," Sergeant Jones said. "I heard some of the others at the station talking about the old routes they walked to keep an eye on known trouble spots. The Fireside Inn was mentioned."

"That was a long time ago," I said. "The place was on its knees when my father bid for it. He turned it around, kicked the troublemakers out, and made it respectable." My father had been far from an angel, but he had a love for community spirit and considered pubs and taverns were the heart of any local community, where people could gather, put their cares aside, and relax after a hard day of work. His shoulders had sometimes brushed against the less refined characters that came with many towns and cities where he made his purchases, but he always kept one step ahead of any trouble.

"Are you certain Florence Sterling was staying at the Fireside Inn?" Inspector Templeton asked.

"Where else would she stay?" Ruby asked breezily. "It was her favourite inn, and she adored Veronica's father. And the Fireside Inn is utterly charming. I like nothing more than sipping a cold martini in front of its roaring fire on a chilly evening."

"We're working, so we won't be drinking," Inspector Templeton said.

"They're the only ones officially on duty," Ruby whispered to me. "We can sneak in a quick snifter before bed."

I smiled, but it was getting late. I was more of a lark than a night owl, and it wouldn't be long before I hankered after my comfortable bed, snuggled beneath the sheets while I read the latest detective novel.

"How are your mother and Matthew?" Inspector Templeton asked me.

"Mother is at death's door, as usual. Although she's been knocking on that door for over a decade, but she keeps being refused entrance. For that, I am eternally grateful."

Inspector Templeton chuckled. "She'll most likely outlive both of us."

"I've no doubt about that. Matthew is getting by. He has good days and bad days. More good, lately, I'm happy to say." My brother had been a casualty of the Great War. He'd served bravely in the Essex Regiment, and although he sustained no serious physical injuries, the mental toll of serving in a brutal war for several years was clear for anyone to see.

"I'll have to drop by, see if I can encourage him out," Inspector Templeton said.

"If you manage it, you're a better woman than me," I said.

Sergeant Jones laughed, but a sharp word from Inspector Templeton silenced him. Inspector Templeton liked Matthew, and having been on active duty himself, he knew about the struggles many of our brave men endured even though it was peacetime.

We stopped outside the Fireside Inn and climbed out. The pub's facade was crafted from rich, dark mahogany wood, its ornate carvings showcasing intricate Art Deco designs. A small, lead-lined glass window adorned with the pub's name allowed a warm light to spill onto the street. Above the entrance, an iron-wrought sign bearing the pub's name swung gently in the breeze, creaking softly with each sway.

A lamppost stood guard near the door, casting a gentle glow over the entrance, welcoming patrons inside. As we approached the door, conversation from customers drifted out.

"I should go in first, to smooth things over," I said.

"What is there to smooth over?" Inspector Templeton asked. "Who's the landlord?"

"Reggie Cole."

He quirked an eyebrow. "I'm sure he's used to visits from the police when things get out of hand."

I hesitated, still reluctant to spring a surprise visit on Reggie. Reggie had been the landlord of the Fireside Inn since my father took it over. If you met Reggie in a dark alley, you'd swiftly walk away, but his sailor tattoos and gruff appearance hid the heart of a true gent. Unfortunately, that true gent had experienced more than a few brushes with the law and thought little of the local coppers.

"We'll go in together," Inspector Templeton said.

I nodded, but took full advantage of Inspector Templeton and Sergeant Jones standing back to let Ruby and me in first with Benji, Quillon still in my arms. The second I was inside, I weaved past tables and dashed to the bar. Reggie stood behind it, holding a glass. His eyes widened when he saw me, then a huge smile broke out across his face, revealing several missing teeth.

"Miss Veronica! What brings you out tonight? And Miss Ruby, always a pleasure." He set down the glass and pressed a hand to his heart.

"I wish I could say we were on a social call." I adjusted Quillon in my arms, and he gave a little whimper. "This is official business."

Reggie's smile faded a fraction, then his gaze lifted over my head, and his eyes narrowed. "You've brought the police?"

"Not for anything you've done." I lowered my voice. "There's been some trouble."

Inspector Templeton reached the bar with Sergeant Jones and cast me an acerbic look. "Reggie Cole?"

He nodded. "What's this about?"

Inspector Templeton made the introductions. "I need to know if you had a guest staying here by the name of Florence Sterling."

Reggie glanced at me, and I nodded at him to answer the inspector.

"She was here," Reggie said. "In fact, when I got five minutes, I planned on heading to her room to clear it. She's overstayed and hasn't paid her bill yet. Which isn't like her. Come to think of it, I haven't seen her since last night."

I let out a soft sigh of relief. My hunch had paid off. "What time did Florence leave here yesterday?"

"If you don't mind, I'll ask the questions," Inspector Templeton said.

I bowed my head in a show of obedience. A show I had no plans to perform in.

"If you could answer the question," Inspector Templeton said to Reggie.

Reggie grated out a laugh. "Miss Sterling left here around five o'clock. She called down for an early dinner, although she ate little of the beef and ale pudding I served her. She was talking about her performance at the Winter Garden and how excited she was."

"That was the last time you saw her?" Inspector Templeton asked.

Reggie nodded. "She strutted into the bar in a posh white dress with feathers and sparkles all over it. She may have been getting on in years, but she was still a sight for sore eyes. I wished her good luck, and she left with her little dog. Do you know when she's coming back? I'd hate to toss her things, but I need the room for other guests. Got a crew of dockers needing a place."

"That's why we're here," I said. "I'm sorry to say, Florence won't be coming back."

"Oh! What should I do with her things?" Reggie glanced at the police but focused on me when he spoke. "Then there's the bill that needs settling."

"I'll deal with that," I said. "Did Florence take the same room as always?"

"She did, the good old girl. Up the stairs, second room on the right. She liked the back room because it was quieter and the peace helped her to focus before her shows."

"Thanks, Reggie." I led the way this time and took everyone up the wooden stairs behind the bar and to the room used by Florence.

"I'll go in first," Inspector Templeton said. "There could be evidence that shouldn't be disturbed."

I stepped back, but stood firm. "I understand you have a job to do, but I own this establishment jointly with my family, so I need to check nothing has been damaged or taken."

"Don't use that as an excuse to poke around." Inspector Templeton reached for the handle but when he tried it, the room was locked, so I dashed back down to the bar and grabbed the spare key from Reggie.

Inspector Templeton unlocked the door and pushed it open. The room featured simple, functional furniture. A sturdy iron bedframe stood against one wall, with a clean patchwork quilt on it. Beside the bed, a small wooden nightstand held a brass lamp, and a well-worn wooden chair was placed in the corner near the dressing table. The wallpaper, though showing its age with a few faded spots and scuffs, was a floral pattern of muted pastels.

Inspector Templeton and Sergeant Jones entered first, while I waited in the corridor with Ruby and the dogs.

"It's a stroke of luck Florence didn't deviate from her routine," Ruby whispered to me.

"I had a hunch she wouldn't. I wouldn't have much enjoyed spending the night behind bars for lying to the police," I murmured in return, gently stroking Quillon.

"You can come in, so long as you're careful," Inspector Templeton said. "Only one of you. And I don't want the dogs in here."

"We can't leave Ruby to lurk in the corridor," I said. "Someone may think she's up to no good."

She tittered. "I'll be on my best behaviour. We'll stay by the door and won't make a peep."

Inspector Templeton nodded, his focus on his new surroundings.

I passed Quillon to Ruby and entered the room, making sure Benji sat beside her, too. There were clothes tossed onto the bed and a small suitcase set open on the floor with a riotous variety of expensive clothing inside. There were also several pairs of high-heeled shoes, and cosmetics were scattered on the dressing table.

Inspector Templeton was leaning over paperwork on the bed, reading through it.

"What have you got there?" I asked.

He didn't look up. "Paperwork on a film deal collaboration and an acting school."

I joined him by the bed and studied the paperwork. "It looks like Florence was setting up her own production company. Good for her. Is this fan mail?"

"More like the scribblings of an obsessed individual," Inspector Templeton said. "A man named Charles is declaring his love for Florence."

"There's a suspect for you," Ruby said from her position by the door. "Some fans can get unhealthily obsessed. I read in the newspaper the other week about a music hall star who was chased by a man who was convinced they should marry!"

"We'll look into him," Inspector Templeton said.

"That bottle of perfume on the dresser is expensive," Ruby said. "It's Habanita. It smells like honey. I've often admired its amber colour when standing outside Harrods. I'm waiting for one of my many generous admirers to buy me a bottle."

"Perhaps one of Florence's admirers bought it for her," I said. "He splashed out on expensive gifts, expected something in return, and when she refused him, he grew unpleasant."

"That's speculation, not facts," Inspector Templeton said.

"We have to start somewhere," I said. "There's plenty to go on here."

"*We* don't have to do anything." He finally looked up from the paperwork, and the stern set of his face would have made a lesser woman tremble. "You're here because the victim rented a room in your inn. Otherwise, you'd be politely asked to leave."

I crossed my arms over my chest. "And I would politely refuse you. If we're settling on pedantic points, I could make you leave, since I own this building."

Before Inspector Templeton retorted his no doubt surly response, footsteps hurried towards the door, and a woman of around fifty with red-rimmed puffy eyes appeared.

Her gaze was full of surprise as it skittered over us. "Oh, my! What are you all doing in here?"

Chapter 6

Inspector Templeton strode to the startled looking woman and introduced himself. "I'm leading the investigation into what happened to Florence Sterling. And you are?"

The teary-eyed woman took a step back, her shaking hand going to her chest, pressing against the lapel of her sensible tweed suit. "Kathleen Buchanan. I was Florence's assistant."

"I remember you! You travelled with Florence to her performances." I ignored Detective Templeton's glare as I joined him by the door. "You won't recall who I am, but I'm Veronica Vale. My father, Davey Vale, owned the Fireside Inn."

"Veronica! Of course, I remember you, although you were a child the last time I saw you. Florence adored staying at the Fireside Inn." A smile wavered across Kathleen's face. She looked at Quillon. "Is that Florence's dog?"

"Yes! We're looking after him," Ruby said. "And his brother. Veronica is always championing the animals. I honestly believe she likes them more than people."

"Most people," I admitted. "I find they have better manners."

"That's very good of you," Kathleen said. "I remember your father liked Quillon and Peregrine."

"He did. And he loved having Florence stay here," I said. "I'm so sorry for your loss. You must have worked with Florence for many years."

"It's the only job I've known," Kathleen said, the words catching in her throat. "I can't believe this has happened."

Detective Templeton's expression suggested he wanted to shove me out of the nearest window for interfering, but I persevered. "Are you also staying here?"

"No, I have an aunt who lives close by, so I've been with her. She's not well, so I visit when I can. Once Florence was settled and everything unpacked, she liked to be on her own before each performance." Kathleen drew in a shaky breath and dabbed her eyes with a well-used handkerchief. "I've come to collect her things. I didn't realise the police would be here."

"Nothing can be taken from this room," Inspector Templeton said.

Kathleen startled. "May I ask why? Nothing bad happened here. From what little I've been told, Florence was found at the Winter Garden Theatre."

I nodded. "She was. But there could be evidence—"

"Thank you, Miss Vale," Inspector Templeton said. "Miss Buchanan, you'll be able to remove Florence's belongings once we've examined the room."

"Please be careful with her things. She was particular about how they were handled. She had so many beautiful vintage items of clothing. And she spent a fortune on shoes. I should know, I used to settle her bills every month. I always told her she needed more forgiving footwear as she matured, but she laughed off my suggestion. Florence said when she lost interest in being glamourous, she'd turn up her toes." Kathleen sniffed back more tears.

"Let's go down to the bar and have a drink," I said. "You must still be in shock."

"I don't drink. Well, only a sweet sherry during the holidays."

"Reggie will serve us anything we like," I said. "We'll leave the police to do their important work while we take care of you."

Before Inspector Templeton could protest, I hurried Kathleen out of the room, and Ruby and I took her to the bar with the dogs. There was a private meeting room tucked at the back of the building, which I commandeered, letting Reggie know we were not to be disturbed. I knew my way around the kitchen, so I swiftly brewed tea, then joined Ruby, the dogs, and Kathleen in the small, tidy room.

Kathleen appeared more composed once settled in a seat, and gratefully took the strong cup of tea I presented her with. "I apologise for being so upset. I was only Florence's employee, but we were together for so long that she felt like family. Everywhere she went, I joined her. I got to see some incredible places, thanks to Florence."

"She led a rich life," Ruby said, the pug comfortably settled on her lap.

"Yes, we travelled to America and parts of Europe, but she always loved her performances in this country. She said England was home."

I settled into a hardbacked chair next to Ruby. "Florence was raised in London, wasn't she?"

Kathleen nodded. "She was proud of her working-class roots and would do free shows in places famous people ignored once they'd gone up in the world. Not Florence. She stayed true to her roots."

"I noticed some paperwork in her bedroom. Florence was establishing a theatre and acting school to help regenerate the East End," I said. "That must have made many people happy. New jobs and education."

"I imagine so, although I don't deal with that side of her work. I was here to make sure Florence got everything she needed. I ensured her outfits were perfect, her diary up-to-date, and her meals as they should be. She had a particular way of doing things and a set routine. My focus was on making sure that never fell apart." Kathleen sipped her tea. "And, of course, I helped with her dogs. Walks, grooming, carrying them when Florence wore an expensive outfit."

"You must be fond of them," I said. "We rescued this little one from the theatre, and I'm fostering Peregrine until we have space at the dogs' home. Perhaps I don't need to concern myself with that. You could take them home."

"They're sweet little things, but they were Florence's, not mine. And I found the walks in the middle of winter unpleasant. Florence walked them when the weather was fine, but otherwise, it was my responsibility. I won't miss that duty."

"Are you sure you can't find space for them?" Ruby asked. "This one's been no trouble since we picked him up. All he wants to do is snuggle and sleep."

"I don't know what I'd do with them during the day. I'll have to find another job now Florence is gone." Her head lowered. "I don't know what to do, though. I've known Florence since we were children. We grew up in the same place. I was working an awful job in a domestic role when Florence got her first acting break. The second she could afford to, she pulled me out and hired me as her assistant. She trained me to run her life. How am I supposed to unlearn that and start again?"

"You have marvellous transferable skills," Ruby said. "Anyone who needs help to organise their life will find you valuable. If I could afford to hire you, I would."

"That's kind of you to say," Kathleen said. "But I'm too old to change. I'm only a few years younger than Florence."

"It sounds like you were content in your role as her assistant," I said.

"More so, recently. Ever since Florence semi-retired, we've been touring less. I found the travel tiring. And of course, now the war is over, we're not venturing into dangerous territory. Not that I had any objections doing that, but I'll admit to being nervous about crossing the water to support the troops. It's an experience I'll never forget."

"Florence did incredible work during the war," I said.

"She always enjoyed a challenge." A sad smile crossed Kathleen's face. "She also had a soft spot for a handsome man in uniform."

Ruby tittered. "Don't we all? There's something about a soldier's uniform that gives them extra handsome points. I also have fond memories of being overseas."

Kathleen looked up. "You served?"

"We both did." I discreetly nudged Ruby. The less we talked about that, the better. "What have the police told you about Florence's death?"

"Since I'm not family, they've revealed barely any details. Of course, I knew there was a problem when I came here this morning and found Florence's room unoccupied. She was never an early riser, so I knew she hadn't gone out for a walk. I asked the landlord, and he said he hadn't seen her since yesterday evening."

"It was unusual for her to change her plans?" I asked.

"Florence had a strict routine when performing. She would celebrate afterwards with select friends, then spend time removing her makeup and her wig and changing her clothing, that sort of thing."

"Did she always do that alone, or did you help?"

"Always alone. Florence insisted on quiet time. It was her time of contemplation, when she could review her performance and calm herself so she'd get a good night of sleep."

"What would Florence do after she finished her quiet time?"

"Depending on the venue, she'd either get a car to take her to her rooms or she'd walk if the distance was short. She preferred to walk because it gave the dogs some exercise."

"The police mentioned she used a car to return here," I said. "Would you consider that unusual, since we're so close to the theatre?"

"It's a little strange," Kathleen said after a few seconds of consideration. "Florence would loath me saying this, but she wasn't getting any younger. She had aches and pains the same as all of us. And those high heels! You most likely saw them in her room. She loved them, and this is a secret I should take to my grave, but she had terrible feet. Florence even had surgery on her bunions because they became so painful. She wore spectacular shoes at last night's performance, so her feet must have been troubling her."

Kathleen's description of Florence's routine tallied with what the theatre manager had told the police.

"In Florence's room upstairs, I noticed fan mail. Did she get a lot of that?" I asked.

"Not so much lately, but certainly in her heyday. She had very determined fans. Some even sent extravagant gifts."

"Was the Habanita perfume a gift?" Ruby asked.

"No, that was her new favourite scent. She would buy herself a fresh bottle of fragrance every month. Florence was an independent woman. Despite having a weakness for a handsome face, she'd say a lady needed to be able to look after herself and not rely on a man for happiness."

"That's an excellent motto to live by." My gaze flicked to my bare ring finger. I should have paid attention to that motto earlier in my life.

Kathleen nodded, but I didn't miss the flicker of sadness in her eyes. "I've always been so busy with Florence, I never had the opportunity to marry. Still, I've led a full and interesting life thanks to her. I have a lot to be grateful about."

There was a pause, where we drank tea and Quillon snuffled in his sleep. Benji was being his usual good boy and had settled by my feet, his tail draped over my shoes.

"I suspect you already have an inkling, but it's likely Florence's death wasn't from natural causes." There was no easy way to say this to Kathleen, but she seemed like an astute, sensible lady.

"I thought as much." Her voice came out shaky. "Too many police and questions being asked to have been anything else. Do you know what happened to her?"

"We can't say too much," I said, "but they found Florence in her dressing room at the Winter Garden Theatre. The police believe it to be foul play."

Kathleen closed her eyes, and tears trickled down her cheeks. "Such a cruel thing to do to such a vivacious woman. Florence brought every room alive when she entered it. Women wanted to be her, and men wanted to be with her. She was a beautiful, talented magnet, drawing people to her."

"That could have made some people jealous," Ruby said. "Perhaps Florence argued with someone. Maybe a jealous fan? Perhaps the person who wrote her that recent letter. There was one in her room."

"The fans were respectful. And although some of the letters contained saucy comments now and again, which Florence used to delight in making me read out because it made me blush, they weren't an issue." Kathleen peered into her cup, her forehead furrowed like a bunch of scrunched silk.

"But there was someone in Florence's life you didn't approve of?" I asked.

"Florence was always generous with her time. She never forgot how tricky the theatre business could be, especially when you're a beautiful young woman starting out with no support. She liked to reach down and offer a hand to rising stars," Kathleen said. "Her most recent recruit is a striking young woman called Eleanor Dixie. She is every bit as beautiful as Florence, but I never cared for her attitude. She assumes she knows it all and could be rude to Florence."

"They were fighting?" I asked.

"The other night, I walked in on them having a right set to. I can't tell you what it was about because they stopped the second I arrived. Eleanor stormed off, and Florence refused to talk about it." Kathleen drew in a breath. "Eleanor is a headstrong young thing and acts on impulse. Florence had been considering asking her to leave. Life as a successful theatre performer requires nerves of steel and a level head. Eleanor possesses neither of those qualities, and her beauty will only take her so far."

"I imagine Eleanor wasn't happy to learn Florence planned to remove her patronage. A recommendation from the amazing Florence Sterling would take a person a long way in their career." Ruby's lips were pursed as she caught my eye.

There was a knock on the door, and a second later, Inspector Templeton appeared. "Miss Buchanan, you are free to collect Florence's things. We've finished our inspection of the room."

"Thank you. I know she would have hated her things to be abandoned. She adored her heels." Kathleen stood, nodded a goodbye to me and Ruby, and left.

"Did you find anything of value in the room?" I asked Inspector Templeton.

"I could ask you the same thing. I assume you weren't discussing knitting patterns over your tea."

I delivered him my fiercest glare. "Perhaps we were. Perhaps we've also realised the game is afoot."

"Murder isn't a game." He sighed. "But I admit, something odd happened to Florence Sterling. Something unnatural."

My nod was curt. "She was murdered, leaving her precious, heart-broken pugs behind. And we intend to find out why."

Chapter 7

"Bring the butter, too," my mother called from her bedroom. "Matthew always forgets it. That boy would eat dry toast if I let him."

I checked the time and repressed a sigh. I was fortunate my uncle Harry ran the newspaper I worked for, because I would be late today. Even though I abhorred lateness, I always made time for my family. I grabbed the china butter container and set it on the tray alongside my mother's usual breakfast of a small bowl of porridge, a pot of stewed tea, which was exactly how she liked it, and several slices of toast. For a woman who barely moved from her bed, she had a hearty appetite.

Matthew ambled into the kitchen, his hair looking like he'd been recently electrocuted and his pyjama top misbuttoned as usual. Without saying a word, he picked up the breakfast tray and took it into our mother's bedroom.

I followed with Benji, a cup of tea in one hand and a slice of buttered toast in the other.

"You can take these away." My mother pushed away the apple slices I'd left for her to enjoy.

I gently pushed them back towards her. Her most recent doctor's visit had concluded with a recommendation she eat more fruit, and she wasn't keen.

"The doctor said an apple every day will do you good." I perched on the end of the bed, with Matthew on the other side. He was already eating a slice of toast meant for Mother.

"I like what I like. I've always eaten this breakfast, even during the war. This routine works for me." Mother tugged her blanket up her chest.

I sighed, not wanting to start the day by bickering. "Where are the pugs?" I'd brought Quillon home last night and reunited him with his brother. They'd been overjoyed to see each other and had been happily settled on the end of my mother's bed the last time I'd seen them.

Matthew chuckled. "From the lumps under the covers, I'm guessing they're in the bed."

"Mother! You're not supposed to have animals under the covers," I scolded. "If you roll on one of them in your sleep, you could get a nasty bite."

"These adorable little creatures would never bite me. And if they did, their teeth are so small, I'd barely notice." Mother flipped back the covers to reveal the pugs fast asleep, as if they'd spent their entire life in my mother's bed. They looked as content as a kitten after a bellyful of its mother's milk.

"Don't get too attached. They're not staying," I said. "You always say we don't have the room."

"I don't want them to stay! I don't like any animals in the house. All the noise, fur, and smells. It does horrors to my nerves." She stroked Peregrine's head, affection shining in her eyes.

I looked at Matthew and shook my head in exasperation. My mother loved to complain about the animals, but she'd be lost without them. And her excuses never held up. The house was far too big for us. It had been too big when my father was alive and used an entire downstairs room as his office. Or, as he liked to call it, his *War Room*. He'd be in and out of there all hours of the day and night, making deals, shaking hands, and figuring out which building to purchase next. I missed the hustle and bustle of his never-ending energy.

"Have you figured out what happened to the pugs' owner?" Matthew asked. "Mother spent most of yesterday evening telling me what Florence had been in. I think I remember her now."

"It's a work in progress," I said. "And I met Inspector Templeton yesterday. He was reluctant to give me the details, but when I shared information, he opened up a fraction."

"Such a nice young man, and so handsome," my mother said. "We must invite him for dinner when my nerves recover."

"According to you, your nerves will never recover, which means he'll never get an invitation," I said. "Good thing, too. Inspector Templeton was less than happy to discover me asking questions of Florence's assistant. But I couldn't let the opportunity pass to winkle out some suspects. Kathleen knew Florence inside and out. She was heartbroken by the loss."

"Suspects?" Matthew tilted his head. "You think someone murdered Florence Sterling?"

My mother flapped her hand in the air. "No talk of murder, it sets my heart fluttering. What did you find out?"

I resisted the desire to roll my eyes and instead finished my toast, taking my time to chew, then fed Benji the crust. "Florence Sterling's body was still at the Winter Garden Theatre when I collected Quillon. And her death was no accident."

"You saw her body?" Matthew grimaced, and his already pale cheeks flushed out their colour, leaving him ghost white.

"Briefly. Although I was focused on ensuring Quillon was safe. It just so happens I saw a few other things while doing so."

"I don't like the sound of this," my mother said. "Was there any blood?"

Matthew and I exclaimed, 'Mother' at the same time. She always feigned disinterest, but in reality, was intensely curious about everything.

I looked at the time and jumped up. "If I don't hurry, I'll lose my job."

"Uncle Harry would never be so cruel," my mother said. "He owed it to this family to provide you with useful employment, especially with his dear brother gone."

I arched an eyebrow as I reached the door. "I hope he employed me out of more than pity."

"Go knock them dead," Matthew said. "Well, they're already dead when you write about them. So, I guess, I mean, write them alive? Err ... do you know what I mean?"

"I understand." I chuckled as I grabbed my coat and buttoned myself in as my family good-naturedly bickered with each other. Then I dashed out the door with Benji. I could still hear my mother berating Matthew as I closed it. As much as I adored my family, I appreciated the time away from the chaos.

I'd had my job as an obituary writer at the London Times ever since the war ended. My uncle Harry, my father's brother, had the same entrepreneurial spirit as my late father. They'd even bought a few pubs together, but Uncle Harry's first love was always looking into stories and digging up evidence, so it was only natural he got into the business of news. And although he printed the occasional scandalous story, his paper was well regarded, and he was often able to get access to influential figures when there was an important story to break.

My work as an obituary writer was not glamourous, but I got satisfaction from it. Dealing with grieving friends and family members took its toll, but writing a well-rounded view of a person's life, focused on their achievements and legacy, was a worthy endeavour.

The newspaper offices were a twenty-minute fast walk from the house, which was perfect, since it gave me time to clear my head, get some exercise, and walk Benji. I was speed walking that morning, since a thick fog swirled through the air, dampening my hair and coat.

I hurried into the office, greeted Mavis, the receptionist, and was pleased to see I was only fifteen minutes late. I quickly took off my coat, repaired my hair, and was about to settle at my desk when Robert

'Bob' Flanders strolled over, a smug look on his face, revealing a hint of cigarette-stained teeth.

Bob was one of our senior reporters and had a ridiculously old-fashioned opinion that a woman's place was in the home. He also liked to remind me regularly that the only reason I had this job was because I was related to the man who owned the newspaper.

"Late again, Veronica." Bob lounged against my desk, the rumpled crotch of his cheap suit in my eye line.

I turned away from him. "Trouble on the trains."

"You walk here! And I can tell you did today, because you're still red faced."

"Very observant. You should put that in a news report. *'World-class obituary writer, a few minutes late for work.'*"

"Fifteen minutes late."

"I didn't realise you were keeping tabs on me."

"Someone has to. Your uncle Harry lets you run around and show up whenever you like."

I spun in my seat and stood. Unfortunately, I was nowhere near eye level with Bob, since he was a tall man, and I stood five foot, three inches without heels. "Have I ever turned in my work late?"

He shrugged. "Most likely."

I jabbed a finger in his chest. "Not even once. Has anyone ever complained about my work?"

"There have been grumblings around the office. You're not qualified for this job. There are good men out there. Men who served in the war, who could do this job much better than you."

"I served too! Have there been any complaints from readers about the quality of my obituaries?" Hidden in my desk was a folder of thank you cards and notes from appreciative family members. I never skimped on the details, always took time to talk to the family, and often worked late to ensure things were perfect.

"You make the dead sound like saints, so of course you won't get complaints," Bob said. "That's bad journalism. Although writing about corpses is hardly a talent worth showing off."

"You believe I should write about the dead's failures?"

"News is news. You shouldn't sugarcoat it. If I were in charge, I'd demote you to trolley dolly. Better yet, fire you and give your position to someone more deserving. A war hero."

"Then it's a good job you aren't in charge, Bob." Uncle Harry strode out of his office, his tie slung over one shoulder and the top button of his white shirt open. "Get back to your desk. You owe me five hundred words on the union rumours."

Bob mumbled an apology and hurried away.

Uncle Harry was a stocky, short guy. He looked very much like my father, with fair hair and dark eyes. Only two years separated them in age, Harry being the older brother.

He fed Benji his usual biscuit and then glanced my way. "Trouble with your mother?"

"No, she's fine. Trouble with my timekeeping, which you know I despise. Early is on time. Sorry. It won't happen again," I said.

"You get your work done, and that's all I care about."

"I do have a favour to ask, though. I'd like to lead on the obituary for Florence Sterling."

Uncle Harry inspected my pile of work. "I heard she died. Suspicious death by the sound of things."

"Possibly. And she was a friend of the family, so it's only right I cover it."

"That's pushing things a bit. I remember your dad saying something about Florence staying at one of your pubs and charming the landlord with her songs. That hardly makes you best pals."

"The Fireside Inn. She rented a room there. And her final performance was at the Winter Garden Theatre."

"I know all about it. My old mate at the station filled me in this morning over eggs and bacon. I've got no problem with you writing her obituary, but stay out of Bob's way. Florence may have been a fading star, but she was a people's favourite. Bob is running a feature on her. A whole page. Stay out of that."

"I promise I'll stay as far away from Bob as I can."

"Best thing to do. I'll stop by and see your mother later, and see if I can encourage Matthew down the pub. He's turned me down five times."

I kissed his cheek. Uncle Harry was always looking out for us. "I wish you the very best of luck."

I was happy now I'd lined up the obituary write-up for Florence. It gave me the perfect reason to question those closest to her and find out who wanted her dead and what they were looking for in her dressing room. My first task was to set up meetings, and I knew exactly who to speak to. I found the telephone number for Kathleen Buchanan and dialled it.

She answered after a few rings.

"Kathleen, it's Veronica Vale. We met yesterday at the Fireside Inn."

"Of course. How may I help?"

"I wanted to let you know I'm writing Florence's obituary for the newspaper I work for. The London Times."

"I didn't know you were a reporter."

"Yes. It's a new position, but I enjoy it. Could you arrange for me to meet with those who were closest to Florence, particularly people at her last performance? I'm sure they'll have wonderful stories to add a sparkle to her obituary. I want to do Florence proud."

"I can do you one better than that. We're meeting back at the Winter Garden Theatre tonight. The police have opened certain areas now Florence's body has been taken away. We're gathering to pay our last respects. Florence so loved the Winter Garden Theatre. You'd be welcome to join us."

"Perfect. What time?"

Kathleen gave me the details, and I made sure she included Ruby's name on the guest list.

Buoyed by my progress, I got stuck into my work, and the rest of the day flew by. I barely had time to stop for lunch and telephone Ruby to let her know we were out that evening and to dress conservatively. No feathers or frills.

When five o'clock rolled around, I took a few minutes to freshen up, before walking with Benji to the Winter Garden Theatre. The police were gone, and the building stood in its grandeur, overlooking a bustling street, the billboards shouting out details of the new shows, all musical comedies.

Ruby was waiting outside the main doors. She wore an appropriately somber black coat over a smart suit with a fitted skirt, meaning she'd come straight from work.

We entered the lobby, and a smartly dressed usher checked our names off a guest list. Then we moved into a private room set off to the side of the main lobby. We accepted glasses of champagne and looked around. The room was decorated in the French style with framed billboard posters of previous shows, many of them signed by the actors.

"I say we split up and listen to any gossip," Ruby whispered to me. "See what people are saying about the dearly departed Florence."

"Good idea." I wandered away, with Benji by my side. Everyone was respectfully quiet, but I overheard several whispered conversations. I'd paused by a group of three people who were talking about Florence's final performance, when I spotted Kathleen waving at me.

She hurried over. "I'm glad you could make it. I'll introduce you."

"Oh! There's no need—"

"Everyone, if I could have your attention. I'd like to introduce you to Veronica Vale."

I cringed as the whispering stopped. So much for being inconspicuous and gathering information. I smiled and nodded at everyone as they stared at me.

"Veronica is writing Florence's obituary for the London Times. She will want to talk to you all, so be sure to spare a few minutes to tell her how wonderful Florence was."

The group murmured, although some of their gazes were suspicious.

"Who would you like to start with?" Kathleen turned to me.

"Perhaps Florence's husband," I said.

"Current husband or ex-husband?"

"Current."

"Perfect. The former Mr Florence Sterling isn't here. And what about her boyfriend?"

I sucked in a breath. "Florence led a colourful lifestyle."

"Some would say it was scandalous," Kathleen said with a shy smile. "I'll show you to the room I prepared, and then bring in Hank. It's best to speak to him before he becomes too sozzled and starts blathering nonsense."

I drew back my shoulders. This evening had become much more eventful than I'd anticipated.

Chapter 8

"Let's start with the basics about Florence and then move on to her death," I said to Ruby as we waited in the small, comfortably furnished room Kathleen had set up for us. "That should make Hank relax."

Ruby sidled around the room, the walls lined with pictures of theatre performers. "We'll start with compliments about Florence's shows."

"I should ask most of the questions. You play the part of my helpful assistant."

Ruby looked heartily offended as she lifted a small silver award from a shelf. "That's Benji's job! We're co-writers. We share things equally."

I grinned at my ever-feisty friend. "Then we're co-writers, but I can't promise you a byline on the obituary."

"I should ask for one. And payment from your uncle, too."

"I'll treat you to a cake from the bakery on Exmouth Street when this is over," I said.

"And then dancing afterwards at the club? I'll need to work off that cake. My figure is not as forgiving as it used to be." Ruby pinched her slender waist. "Nobody told me that turning thirty would lead to me getting the figure of an old maid."

"You're far from an old maid. Heads turn wherever you go."

"Not the right heads, though. I still attract the cads."

The door opened, and Kathleen appeared. Beside her was a strikingly handsome man of around forty with slicked-back dark hair, wearing an open-necked shirt and smartly pressed black trousers. "This is Hank Monroe, Florence's husband."

Kathleen introduced us, while Ruby swiftly took her seat. Hank strolled over and shook our hands, but my attention was diverted by Kathleen discreetly miming that he'd been drinking. I nodded a thanks for the warning as she closed the door.

"You're here to write about my wonderful old girl, I hear." Hank sank into an easy chair and took a sip from the glass of champagne he'd brought with him.

"That's right," I said, glancing at Ruby. "We specialise in writing obituaries."

He shook his head. "I never thought I'd be sitting here talking about my wife's death. She always seemed so full of life. You'd never think she was as old as she was. And Florence loved to tease reporters by changing her year of birth. She once accidentally made herself a decade younger."

I slid a slim black notepad from my handbag and set it on the table. "You don't mind if I make a few notes while we talk?"

"Go right ahead," Hank said. "But make sure Florence sounds like the angel she was. We had exciting times together, and I want everyone else to think as fondly of her as I do."

"You look familiar," Ruby said. "Are you in theatre, too?"

"I'm an actor. I started out in theatre, but I'm interested in moving pictures. I've starred in a few things. I played a dashing pilot in my last production."

"No, not film," Ruby said. "Did you model for that advertisement for coal tar soap?"

His cheeks flushed. "I forget. I'm given so much work that I don't know where I am from one day to the next. I'm most interested in films, though. There's talk of me heading to Hollywood if things go well."

"How exciting," Ruby said. "Florence must have been delighted for you."

"You'd think, but she became a homebody as she aged. She always adored London. I can't think why, though. All the damp and grey. America seems much more glamourous."

"I'm sure it has its charms," I said. "Is that how you met Florence? You performed together?"

Hank smiled and shook his head. "I was a fan! I idolised Florence from afar. I used to go to all her shows. I must have seen the film she was in, Wingspan, a dozen times. She was a mature beauty, but it was her presence that enchanted me. So much energy and passion in everything she did."

"If you were only a fan, how did you come to be her husband?" I asked.

"I snuck into an after-show gathering. You get to know where the back entrances are in theatres and cinemas after a while. I got inside and pretended I was one of her guests. Florence noticed me. I thought I was in real trouble when she drew me to one side and asked what I was doing at her exclusive party. She knew every guest, and I most definitely wasn't on her list. I confessed my admiration, and do you know what she did?"

"I'm guessing she didn't toss you onto the street, or have you arrested," I said.

"She laughed. Florence's laugh was something else. She got me a glass of champagne and made me tell her my life story. I was star struck. To begin with, I fumbled my words and blushed like a young lad. But she put me at ease. Sure, she was glitz and glamour in front of the cameras, but Florence was down-to-earth. Neither of us came from money, so she understood my ambitions."

"And you fell in love just like that?" Ruby asked.

"We were friends first. Florence had a good heart. If she saw someone was genuine but struggling, she'd help them. She always had people under her wing and looked out for them to make sure they didn't get in any trouble." He swigged most of the glass of champagne. "Believe me, it's easy to do in this cutthroat business."

"Were you one of those she mentored?" I asked.

"To begin with, but we quickly grew close. I used to help her run lines, and she could see I had talent. Florence got me my first acting job. It was nothing special, but it gave me a foot in the door, and I exploited it every chance I got."

"It sounds like you want bigger things than bit parts in Florence's films," I said.

"A man needs ambition. I'd have never been able to keep up with Florence if I didn't have it."

Ruby continued chatting to Hank about the films he'd been in, while I made a pretence of reading through my notes. There was a motive here. Hank may have been fond of Florence, but there was no sign of a husband grieving the loss of his beloved wife. Perhaps he'd demanded bigger roles in the films or more money, so he could try his luck in America, and Florence had denied him.

"Do you know what plans Florence made for her estate?" I asked. "Given how charitable she was, I'd imagine she hoped her work would continue. I'd like to include any information about her good deeds in the obituary."

Hank smirked and rolled his almost empty champagne glass between his hands. "If you're asking if I get everything, the answer is no. Florence was shrewd. We had a legal agreement to ensure everything was fair. I met Florence when she was at the top of her game, so it was no surprise when she suggested we see a legal chap to make sure she wasn't exploited. Not that I would have done anything so ungentlemanly, but Florence met plenty of types who wanted something from her."

"You had no problem with such an agreement?" I asked.

"Why should I? I didn't marry Florence for her money. I don't know what she's left me, but I'll get something. She said she'd always look after me. Not that I'm worried. I'll be off to America soon and see my own name in lights. Then I'll be the one fending off the gold diggers."

"Florence had no children, did she?" Ruby asked.

"No, her career was her first love. She travelled a lot, and all the late-night performances meant it was hard for her to find time for a family," Hank said.

"She never wanted them?"

"By the time we met, the option wasn't there to be discussed." Hank ducked his head. "I'm no expert on a lady's reproductive system, though, but she was moving into her golden years."

The subject clearly made Hank uncomfortable, so I moved on to a safer topic. "What about her previous husband?" I checked through the notes I'd made in the office. "Clint Brewster. Does he still live in London?"

"He moved away a long time ago. Headed down to Devon, I believe. And on Florence's purse. You see, she still looks after people, even though they no longer feature in her life. Although, they were still friendly. They exchanged cards and notes, and Florence always remembered his birthday."

I made a note to check Clint's whereabouts at the time of Florence's murder.

"If you don't mind me asking, these questions are odd. I figured you'd want to know about Florence's highlights and what she'll be remembered for." Hank's gaze narrowed. "You're not looking for an angle, are you? I won't have Florence's good name smeared for a salacious bit of scandal."

"We absolutely need all of this information," Ruby said smoothly. "It's important for context. Florence lived a full life, so we need to cover everything. And we don't want to offend anyone important by leaving them out."

"It seems to me you're poking around because you want to figure out what actually happened to her." Hank arched an eyebrow. "That would be a scoop. Might get you off the boring old obituary desk and writing genuine stories."

I bristled at the less than veiled insult. "I'm perfectly content writing people's obituaries. It's good to provide a printed memorial of a person's time on this earth. We all think we have more time than we do to make a difference and improve things, but that's rarely the case. When I find an exemplary person, I ensure the words I write about them shine."

Hank looked momentarily surprised. "Good for you. It must get dull, though. People telling you the same thing over and over again. What a wonderful person the deceased was, how they'll be missed. Never any criticism, since it's wrong to speak ill of the departed."

"You sound like you won't miss Florence," Ruby said.

"She was a decent old lady. Kind to most, and tolerant to those she didn't like. But she always called a spade a spade. No messing around, straight to the point with everything. And there were those she definitely didn't trust."

"Who would that be?" I held my pencil poised, ready to grab a name.

Hank set down his champagne flute and leaned forward, a wry expression on his face. "Florence didn't trust investment types. She didn't like giving them her money. When she first started acting, she insisted on being paid in cash on the day. And she hid that cash. I once found a pile under a mattress. She said it was better there than in the grimy hands of some non-trustworthy man who would spend it on something he shouldn't. She hated bankers. The man she was first engaged to was a banker. Reginald something or other. I suspect that coloured her opinion."

"I didn't find a record of a broken engagement when I researched Florence's background," I said.

"Reginald's dead. Has been for years. He was older than Florence, and I got the impression he dazzled her with his maturity. But she was quick enough to see through him when he pressured her into investing money into his business." Hank glanced around. "The rumour has it, Florence never got over her revulsion for banker types and would hide money all over her houses."

"How much of that money did you find?" Ruby asked.

He chuckled. "Just that one stack. I'm sure Florence only talked about hiding money to test people and see if they were after her for her cash or her friendship."

I sat back in my seat. Perhaps someone thought Florence was telling the truth about storing her money so unwisely. It would explain why her dressing room had been turned over.

"Did you attend Florence's party following her performance at the Winter Garden Theatre?" I asked.

"I was always at her parties. She liked me to be close. She said she needed to keep an eye on me so I didn't drink too much or flirt too hard." Hank snort laughed. "I teased her that I thought the same about her. She was an outrageous flirt."

"If Veronica's father was still alive, he'd tell you a story about Florence," Ruby said.

"Is that so?" Hank cocked his head, his attention on me. "Your family knew Florence?"

"In a way. My family owns the Fireside Inn," I said.

"Oh! Charming place. Florence called it cosy. How fascinating."

"Indeed. What did you do after the party?" I was keen to keep the conversation focused.

"Same as always. I could always tell when Florence had had enough of socialising. She'd get a fixed smile on her face, and her eyes would turn glassy. Stage performing is physically and mentally demanding, and as Florence aged, she struggled to manage," Hank said. "I gently suggested we call it a night, and she made no protests. I walked her to her dressing room, and then left. She shut the door, and I heard the lock turn. It was the last time I saw her."

"You could have been the last person to see her alive," Ruby said, sounding slightly breathless.

"That would have been her killer," Hank said. "It's a damn shame what happened, but for all Florence's shrewdness in certain areas of life, she was naïve about letting people in. I always worried that side of her would be her undoing. Now, here we are." He inspected the empty champagne flute.

"Did everyone leave the theatre at the same time as you?" I asked.

"We trickled out one after the other, around ten thirty." Hank smiled and rubbed his hands together. "I have a fun story you can publish. Let me tell you about when Florence took me to Paris. We visited the Eiffel Tower. I can't see it lasting. Ugly as sin. A giant cone of metal!"

There was a sharp tap on the door, and it opened before I responded. An angry-faced Inspector

Templeton looked in, his gaze narrowing as he saw what we were doing.

Oh, dear. How frightfully irritating. Our interrogation game was up before we were even at the mid-point.

Chapter 9

Inspector Templeton made swift work of removing Hank from the room and then shut the door, trapping us inside. He was still glaring at me while he petted Benji.

I tucked my notepad and pencil away, settled my hands in my lap, and waited for the inevitable scolding.

"You were fortunate to get an invitation to such a privileged gathering," Inspector Templeton said. "And you, too, Ruby. I didn't know you moved in the theatre circles. I thought the horse clique was more your type."

"I'm adaptable. Although, I'll admit to being more comfortable around horses. They never hide their true intentions." Ruby shifted in her seat. "Inspector, I must protest at this intrusion. You interrupted an important interview."

"Horse woman and reporter now. Your talents are never ending." A muscle twitched in Inspector Templeton's jaw. "I suppose, if I checked Veronica's notes, they'd be about Florence's incredible acting career and have nothing to do with her murder."

I gently nudged my handbag with my foot to make it harder for him to grab. "I may have made a few discreet enquiries about the manner of her death. There's no harm in it. We may uncover a useful clue or a new suspect, which we would have been delighted to pass your way."

"Leave the clue hunting and suspect finding to the police," Inspector Templeton said. "We all have our jobs to do. Jobs we are trained for. You won't find me marching into the newspaper office with an article about police reform for your uncle, so I don't expect you to interfere in an active police investigation. We stay in our correct lanes, and no one gets into trouble."

"We're not causing trouble," Ruby said. "We're being helpful."

"I have more than enough help," Inspector Templeton said. "I have a dozen new recruits, all wet behind the ears and in need of monitoring. And now this high-profile murder to deal with. I don't need two thorns in my side stirring up trouble."

"Are we the stirring thorns?" Ruby tutted. "How very dare he? And a mixed metaphor too. It's a good job you don't write the news."

I hid a smile. We'd been called worse. "Make sure to include some training from me about best practices in looking after stray animals for your new recruits."

"I haven't forgotten. And if I do, you'll remind me at every opportunity." Inspector Templeton held out a hand. "Let me see your notes."

"There's no need," I said. "I'm happy to tell you what we learned to move your investigation forward."

Inspector Templeton's cheeks flushed. I couldn't tell if it was due to anger or embarrassment. "I've already spoken to Hank. He was one of the first people I contacted about Florence's death."

"How did he take the news?" I asked. "When we spoke to him, he seemed stoically resigned. There wasn't a tear shed."

"There was plenty of champagne quaffed, though. And did you notice how he kept referring to Florence's age?" Ruby asked. "Old girl, old lady. There's probably a fifteen-year age gap between them, but there's no need to keep pointing it out."

"Twenty years, actually," Inspector Templeton said. "Hank is forty, and Florence was sixty."

"Goodness, it's unusual for a younger, handsome man to fall for a mature woman, no matter how beautiful she once was," Ruby said. "And from Hank's relaxed attitude, it won't be long before he's back on the market looking for his next wife. I wonder who his target will be this time."

"He didn't target Florence," Inspector Templeton said. "They met when he was a struggling actor. She helped him, and they fell in love."

"According to him," I said. "We only spoke to him for ten minutes, and it was clear he didn't love Florence in a romantic sense. Hank may have had respect for her career and a lot of interest in her money to give him a leg up for his push into Hollywood, but that's not a romantic relationship. It's not something to base a marriage on."

"I don't have time for your speculation into romantic love or marriages of convenience," Inspector Templeton said. "People marry for a range of reasons. I'm here to question more suspects, and I can't have you getting in the way."

"I think you mean assisting you in your difficult investigation," I said. "Don't be so quick to dismiss us.

People are more willing to talk to a pair of friendly, sensible-headed women than the police. They're scared if they let their guards down, you'll unearth their deepest secrets and put them behind bars."

"This isn't one of Florence's over-the-top films. We don't drag people off to a mysterious cell and lock them away, never to be heard from again." Inspector Templeton's shoulders were rising by the second. "There are procedures to follow, and you're not following them. And you never will because you aren't part of the police."

"Does that mean if we find useful information during our day-to-day activities, we should keep it to ourselves?" I asked as sweetly as possible, but I couldn't stop a small smile from dancing across my face.

"Gather your things, make your apologies, and leave, before I find out if there really is a cell we can put misbehaving nosy journalists, her dog, and her horse-mad friend in and then handily lose the key for a very long time."

"You'd never do that to Benji," I said.

"Don't test me, Veronica."

That was our cue to leave. We bustled out of the room and informed Kathleen we'd be in touch, all under the stern glare of Inspector Templeton, and then dashed out of the theatre.

"That was so unnecessary." Ruby turned up the collar of her smart coat. "We were doing our job, the same as him. You can use some of the information from Hank in the obituary."

"I'm not sure which part." I set off with Benji at a brisk pace, Ruby hurrying to keep up. "I could write a paragraph about how they met while working together, but Hank wasn't in love with Florence. He was an obsessed fan with a handsome face, who landed on his feet. For whatever reason, Florence fell for his charms. If she was still alive, he'd have continued to exploit her."

"Maybe don't put that in the obituary," Ruby said. "Have we got time for a martini? We can go over your notes and plan our next move."

"Excuse me! Sorry, have you got a moment?"

I turned to see a curvaceous blonde hurrying towards us in a pale coat far too flimsy for the damp evening air.

"I'm sorry to bother you, but we didn't get a chance to speak, and then I saw you leaving. I'm Eleanor Dixie. I was so looking forward to talking to you about Florence."

I kept my composure, although I recognised the name. Eleanor Dixie was Florence's latest star in the making, the protégé who'd argued with her not long before Florence had been killed. "I should be the one to apologise. We forgot an important appointment we must get to."

"Another interview," Ruby said by way of a cover.

"Of course. How exciting, life as a journalist. You're so lucky." Eleanor had striking blue eyes and full lips. I could imagine those looks transferred well into film.

"Is there something I can do for you?" I asked.

"I spent almost every evening with Florence. I'll give you some dazzling obituary quotes, so long as you mention me in the article." She fluttered her beautiful dark lashes. "You know what they say: there's no such thing as bad press."

"You must have gotten to know Florence well, since you spent so much time together," I said.

"We were like best friends and sisters rolled into one," she said. "Maybe tomorrow? You can buy me lunch, and I'll tell you all about Florence. Just make sure you put my full name in the article."

"It's a date." I was excited as we fixed a time and a place to meet. Interviewing Eleanor over a plate of food would give me the perfect opportunity to find out how bad their feuding had become and just how far she'd gone to stop it.

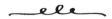

"Veronica, I need a word."

I looked up in surprise at my uncle's stern tone. I'd arrived early to work that morning to make up for my previous lateness, and I'd had my head down all day, working on various obituaries. I'd covered a minor politician, a deceased artist, and I was working my way through the research on a former judge. I set down my pencil, hurried into his office with Benji beside me, and closed the door.

"Take a seat," Uncle Harry said.

"Is something the matter?" I settled into the comfortable chair in the corner of my uncle's office. The smell of cigarette smoke and coffee lingered, and there was an empty bowl of whatever he'd had for breakfast on the desk. The man lived and breathed the news and was always here, often working well past midnight. I'd even caught him sleeping here a time or two when an important story was breaking.

"I've just had a long and uncomfortable conversation with Inspector Jacob Templeton. Could you imagine what that would have been about?" Uncle Harry asked.

I furrowed my brow. "Inspector Templeton doesn't like me. He's rude every time we meet."

"Where did you last meet him? Was it when poking about in things you shouldn't?"

"I was doing my job when he rudely evicted me from the Winter Garden Theatre," I said. "I'd been invited by Florence's assistant to attend an exclusive gathering. It was an ideal opportunity to get quotes about Florence. It would have made for a magnificent piece."

Uncle Harry tucked his fingers behind his head and leaned back so far, I was worried he'd fall off his chair. "With your dad gone, I'm responsible for your well-being."

"As lovely as that is to know, I'm a grown woman. I look after myself."

He shook his head. "I know the world is changing. Women have more rights and more opportunities than ever before, but you're still vulnerable. You get mixed up in things you shouldn't, and it can quickly go wrong."

"I was in no danger yesterday evening," I said. "I was in a respectable venue, and I had Ruby and Benji with me. They're stalwart protectors, and would let nothing bad happen to me."

Benji wagged his tail in agreement.

"I know you girls think you're indomitable, but there are deviant people out there who can't be trusted. We both know what happened to your father."

My heart ached every time someone brought up his death. "Mother never talks about him. Matthew won't, and you rarely do. It sometimes feels as if he never existed."

"Davey had the personality of two flamboyant film stars, so we both know he existed. People remember him. And some of those memories aren't so rosy."

I waited for my uncle to continue.

"And I rarely talk about him because some things are too painful to discuss. But we know the outcome of what happened when he got himself mixed up with the wrong people."

My father's business endeavours had taken him into some of the more downtrodden areas of this country. He'd purchased rundown or failing pubs in and around London, and he'd gone as far as Yorkshire and over to Ireland to find opportunities to invest in. An outsider treading on toes wasn't always popular."I don't want to get into a discussion about this," Uncle Harry said. "But be careful. We are a small family, and I refuse to lose anyone else I care about."

I reached across the desk and held out my hand until he unlaced his fingers and grabbed it, holding it tight.

"We have a good life, a comfortable life. Be happy with that," he said.

"I am. But I refuse to cower from reality, even if it is unseemly. The more I learn about Florence Sterling's death, the more I see there are plenty of people who wanted her dead. When I interviewed Hank Monroe, he revealed Florence hid piles of money in her home. Was she killed because someone wanted that money?"

"If that's the truth, the police will discover it. It's not for you to dig around for a story. Write Florence's obituary and put the rest of the questions out of your mind."

I frowned, my gaze skimming the papers scattered across my uncle's desk. "I'm not nosy because I like getting gossip. But I demand the truth. I abhor unkindness. We all saw too much of that during the war, and if I have an opportunity to stamp it out, I will."

"You have so much, Veronica, don't spoil things," Uncle Harry said. "There are many men who want your job."

I withdrew my hand and glowered at him. "Don't do me any favours by keeping me employed. If you can find someone better to write the stories of the dead, get rid of me. I can manage without your charity."

He made a noise of exasperation. "You are an incredible writer, and I wish I could give you more opportunities to see your name in the newspaper, but the rest of the team would revolt."

I squashed my temper and settled a hand on Benji's head. "I understand. I have no objections about looking after our war heroes and making sure they have jobs, too."

"We look after them, and I look after you. You're the closest thing I have to a daughter, and I feel even more responsible for you now Davy has gone. But please, stop drawing the attention of the police. You don't want to get on their wrong side. Scotland Yard has dug out most of the corruption, but those problems have deep roots and some are still alive. If any flourish, I don't want you standing in the way."

"I'll be careful, I promise." I stood, walked around the desk, and kissed his cheek. "Any interviews will be done in safe spaces with lots of people around me."

"And you'll stick to the obituary writing?"

I crossed my fingers behind my back. "Florence's obituary will be my best work to date."

Uncle Harry shook his head and scratched his fingers across his forehead. "Make sure I get no more calls from the police about you."

"Understood." I dashed back to my desk. I'd just settled in when I realised, I only had twenty minutes to get to my luncheon appointment with Eleanor. I rushed to the powder room to freshen my makeup, before hurrying out with Benji.

I sped along the busy streets, the beeps from automobiles and the bustle of London life surrounding me, revealing a prosperous and safe city, and entered the café after securing Benji to a post outside. I'd have preferred to bring him in with me, but the café owner would have had a few things to say if I did, and Benji was content to watch the world pass, so long as he could see where I was.

Ruby walked in a few seconds later while I was waiting for the waitress to notice me, her cheeks pink. "I was almost running to catch up with you. Didn't you hear me calling your name?"

"Sorry, I was lost in thought." I squeezed her arm in way of a greeting as we announced our names to the server, and they took us to a small table at the back of the café set for four people.

Eleanor was already seated, and she was not alone. An attractive blonde man in his early thirties stood as we reached the table.

"It's a pleasure to meet you both. I'm Dirk Donovan."

Ruby drew in a breath. "The film star and director?"

His smile was dazzling, with a hint of dimple. "You've heard of me?"

We settled into our seats, and the waitress took our drinks order.

"Of course I have," Ruby said. "You directed Anna the Adventuress. It's one of my favourite silent films. And I saw you in several films before you turned to making them. How talented!"

"Co-directed. Do you enjoy the pictures?"

"I adore them," Ruby said. "I can spend all Saturday afternoon at them."

"I hope you don't mind me bringing Dirk along," Eleanor said, a note of apology in her voice. "When he heard we were meeting, he insisted he attend. He saw you with the police at the theatre last night and thought you could help him."

I focused my attention on Dirk. "What makes you think that?"

"Because you have that chap's ear. The inspector paid attention to you. I'm here to set the record straight. I definitely did not kill Florence Sterling."

Chapter 10

I remained calm, even though my heart skipped a beat at how vehemently Dirk announced his innocence. Could it be a guilty conscience making him protest so much?

"We have no sway over the police," Ruby said.

"You have an in with them, though," Dirk said. He paused while our drinks were brought over, and we placed our luncheon orders. I noted Eleanor and Dirk picked the most expensive items on the menu. "I saw how that copper looked at you."

"If you're referring to Inspector Jacob Templeton, he mainly looks at me with suspicion," I said. "Our paths have crossed many times. My work at the London Times means we're often involved in the same cases."

"I told Dirk about your experience as an obituary writer," Eleanor said. "And how you promised I'd feature heavily with my wonderful memories about Florence."

"There will be room for everyone's memories," I said. "The paper is planning a feature on her. She was such a darling of the local theatre groups."

"I must be in that feature, too. Will you be doing the interviews?" Eleanor asked. "You could make it an exclusive. That'll draw readers' interest."

"It's something to consider," I said as diplomatically as possible.

"What did you mean by the way Inspector Templeton looked at Veronica?" Ruby's tone may have been sweet, but she wasn't fooling me. She often teased me over how I could rile Inspector Templeton. She believed he had a fondness for me, which was ridiculous. I irritated him immensely, and he did likewise to me. There was no fondness to be had.

"The newspapers will do you right. You have nothing to concern yourself with." Dirk patted Eleanor's hand. "But it's important they ignore the rumours about me. Tell the police that."

"What would those rumours be?" I flapped my napkin onto my lap.

"Veronica and Ruby aren't part of the theatre crowd," Eleanor said to Dirk. "They won't know what the mean-spirited types have said about you when you moved into production. Tell them! They need to know everything."

I leaned forward, eager to learn what gossip was being spread about Dirk.

"None of it's true. You must understand that," Dirk said.

"Absolutely!" I inched closer.

Dirk lowered his chin. "Vicious tongues have suggested I exploit struggling actresses. As if I'd ever do such a thing. I'm a respectable director. It's the industry that is rotten. It's not my fault they do things a certain way. You can't change an entire business."

"What exploitation are they suggesting you're involved in?" Ruby neatened her cutlery.

"Promising acting jobs in return for ... favours," Dirk said. "It's not polite to talk about the specifics in the company of ladies. And since I don't even want to talk about it, I'd never do it. I'm a retired actor, so I know how situations can become difficult."

Eleanor shifted in her seat. "I've been asked to do dreadful things. I keep thinking I should get married because a ring on my finger would keep away the worst of the predators."

"I'm not sure those with a mind for that kind of thing would care if a woman was married or not," I said.

She sighed and inspected her bare hand, the nails painted a pale pink. "True. And, once you marry, the business sees you differently. They'd cast me as a sensible, ordinary type, not a dazzling star."

"It sounds like a difficult industry to feel safe in," I said.

Dirk thumped a hand on the table, causing several diners to glance our way. "People are saying those dreadful things about me to ruin me. This industry is so full of spite and jealousy. If word gets back to the police that I'm involved in something so terrible, it'll make them question my character and whether I had anything to do with Florence's death. Which I didn't."

Eleanor squeezed his arm. "Have a sip of water. Honestly, he's more theatrical than the actual theatre types. That's method actors for you."

"What's that?" Ruby asked.

Dirk didn't reach for his water but instead took a sip from the cocktail he'd ordered. "I immerse myself into a character. Different clothing, voice, even handwriting! It was effective but tiring."

"Was that why you moved into directing?" I enquired.

He nodded. "Although it's no less tiring. Florence was a good woman, and it was a rotten thing that happened to her. We'd been friends for years. We were about to go into business together. Everything was arranged, just a few bits of paperwork to finish off. Why would I scupper such an incredible opportunity?"

"It would have been the deal of the decade," Eleanor said. "Your combined contacts, Florence's money, and my talent. Perfection!"

"Florence rented a room at the Fireside Inn while performing at the Winter Garden Theatre," I said. "It's a business owned by my family. When I visited her room, I noticed paperwork. That was to do with your deal?"

Dirk nodded. "Most likely. I sent a bundle to a pub so she could look over some changes. Do you know if she signed it? I'm certain she did. We were all excited to start this new venture."

"I didn't get close enough to see it all. The police were with us and wanted to check for anything unusual in the room," I said.

"There you go! I knew you had an in with them." Dirk sighed. "With a signature on the paperwork, I can salvage things. Just because Florence is gone doesn't mean the deal can't go through. A deal is a deal."

"Her estate will have something to say about that," I said.

Dirk waved away my comment as our food arrived. "I won't be defeated. If everything had gone to plan, today would have been the start of something special. I had interviews lined up with agents. Of course, they have been postponed out of respect for Florence."

I took a moment to sample my crab salad as I turned over everything Dirk had told us. There was a motive here. The deal with Florence could have gone wrong. It would be handy to see that paperwork again, but Inspector Templeton wouldn't let me anywhere near it.

"Tell us more about the deal you'd planned," Ruby said. "It sounds fascinating."

Eleanor exhaled on a breathy sigh. "We're making three films, one after the other. Florence, of course, would be in all of them, although we were having a silly debate about what role was most suitable for her."

"She was a talented actress," Ruby said. "I've seen her in lots of performances. In live theatre, too."

"She knew how to work a stage." Dirk cut into his steak. "But we had run into a small complication. Florence wanted the starring roles, and I needed a much younger actress. It caused friction."

"I was to be the star," Eleanor said. "I suggested several roles written for her. She could have been the grandmother, the old spinster, and one of the films involved royalty, so I suggested she be the white-haired Duchess who went crazy. She hated them all. She said her star shone brighter than mine, and her name would bring people to the pictures. I'll have you know, I've been in two soap advertisements. Two!"

Dirk smirked. "I didn't have the heart to tell Florence there was only so much makeup could conceal, and the camera is less forgiving than the stage. With the bright lights and dazzle, it's easy for theatregoers to overlook age, but cameras miss nothing. Florence wouldn't listen to me."

"She was out of touch with the industry," Eleanor said. "And she had nothing to complain about. She would have had a decent role in the films. We wouldn't have left her out."

"It sounds like the films could have made you wealthy," I said.

"We ran the numbers, and Florence was happy with the profit we forecast," Dirk said. "We were just haggling over those wretched cast lists. I thought she'd settled everything. This last show wore her out, and she admitted to feeling tired. She even talked about bringing the tour to an end early."

"Florence would never have done that," Eleanor said. "She loved to please her fans."

"Did you see her final show?" I asked.

"We were there." Dirk took a gulp of his cocktail. "Florence gave us complimentary tickets. It was wonderful. She performed all the old favourites, and her fans loved it. She did her best work twenty years ago."

"You went to the party after the show?" Ruby asked.

"I never miss them. It's the best place to get gossip and, of course, congratulate Florence on an excellent job."

"How did Florence seem at the party?" I asked. "Was she worried about anything?"

"She was distracted because one of her dogs was unwell." Dirk nudged Eleanor, and the smile they exchanged was rue filled. "Those creatures were a nuisance. She was always carrying them around and talking to them as if they were babies."

"One of them even made a grab for the hem of my dress," Eleanor said. "I had to shoo the creature away. But wherever Florence went, those leaping little creatures were there, too. You had to get used to them if you spent time with her. I pretended to like them, but they annoyed me."

I glanced at Benji, who sat happily outside. He saw me looking at him and wagged his tail. It was a mystery how anyone could dislike dogs. They were so loyal.

"There was only one dog at the party, though. Florence's assistant said the other one was left at Florence's enormous old home in Mayfair. Why she still owns it is beyond me." Dirk shook his head. "I kept telling her to give it up. Release the capital so she could make a bigger investment in the production company."

"She didn't like that idea?" I asked.

"Stubborn old girl wouldn't hear about it. She said she'd lived in that house for almost thirty years, and it was full of memories and personal things, so she'd never be able to tear herself away. I tried to entice her to Spain. There's a growing retirement community of faded theatre stars living there."

"She'd have loved the winter sun." Eleanor ate the olive from her martini.

"I never thought of Florence as fading," I said. "Her performances were always high class."

"I'm not saying she didn't have talent, but she needed to step aside for the next generation. She was holding on too tight. It was unbecoming," Dirk said.

"Is that why you think she died?" I deliberately lowered my voice so as not to alarm the other diners as the conversation shifted to the topic of murder.

"I couldn't tell you why she was killed," Dirk said. "All I know for certain is that it had nothing to do with me. Perhaps if she'd had more in her life than theatre and film, she'd have been more relaxed about letting go, letting others fill her shoes and invest her money wisely."

"She had her husband to support her," I said.

"That idiot! He wasn't in the relationship because of love."

"Don't say such a thing." Eleanor swatted Dirk's hand. "Hank did his best."

"Hank saw a golden goose and pinned it down. Florence was too old to move out of the way."

That was an interesting description of their relationship. It had been easy to see Hank cared little for Florence, but had he secretly despised her? Despised her enough to kill her when he'd had enough? It wasn't the first time I'd considered that motive.

"Florence should have had children," Eleanor said. "They could have eased her into her retirement. Given her grandchildren, something else to think about."

"I agree. It's natural for women to want children," Dirk said. "I blame the war. Ever since women were given a false sense of their capabilities when men were sent to do their duty, they've gotten full of themselves."

Ruby sucked in a breath, two red dots colouring her cheeks. I grabbed her hand beneath the table and squeezed hard. We were single, well past a respectable marrying age, and neither of us had children. It was a life few chose, but it suited us well.

"Marriage and children may not be for everybody," I said smoothly. "From what I'm learning about Florence, her first love was her career."

"Like I said, not a natural behaviour for a woman. And to prove my point, look at what happened. Florence died alone in a dressing room late at night in a theatre.

She should have been tucked up in bed with her husband or at home caring for her grandchildren." Dirk finished his steak and pushed his plate away, gesturing to the server for another round of drinks. "Just make sure to put in a good word for me with the police. I refuse to have my name sullied."

"I make no promises," I murmured. "But I shall see what I can do."

"If you need something to sweeten our deal, I can get you a part in a film. Nothing with lines, but it would be fun to do a walk on. You can meet the actors, too." Dirk waggled his neat eyebrows. "Doesn't every woman want to be famous?"

Ruby glanced at me and nodded, hard amusement glittering in her eyes.

I pursed my lips and shook my head. "I prefer the quiet life. So does Ruby."

"I'm sure you ladies would look the part with tweaks from the wardrobe girls. They can make anyone look halfway presentable."

"I prefer this look. If you consider that unpresentable, it's a concern to deal with in your own time."

Dirk yelped and glared at Eleanor. He reached down and rubbed his shin. "I was trying to be helpful! You scratch my back and all that. If you want lines, I can fix something for you. It may end up on the cutting room floor, though."

"I'm content to watch films, not be in them." I composed myself as I sipped my water. The very cheek of the man. I occasionally had fur on my clothes and mud splatter on my shoes, and if my pockets smelled of dog biscuits and sausage, it wasn't a problem that concerned me.

"A life in the limelight isn't for everyone," Eleanor said, in an effort to smooth the tension. "It's good to see the plainer types recognise that they can't have it all."

Ruby almost choked on her drink.

"How long did you stay at the party after the show?" It was an effort to rein in my anger, but I needed to know everything before I never saw Eleanor or Dirk again.

"It was all over by ten thirty." Dirk drained his glass and clicked his fingers at the server. "Where are those drinks? Florence didn't enjoy late nights anymore. Too old, you see. I left with Eleanor."

She nodded. Her gaze shot over my head, and the colour drained from her face. "Oh my goodness. What is he doing here?"

Chapter 11

I twisted in my seat at the same time as Ruby, spotting a tall, skinny man of around forty with a pale face and bushy eyebrows peering in the café window. He was looking at Eleanor. His eyes were red-rimmed, and it looked like he'd slept in his crumpled dark suit.

"Do you know that man?" I asked.

"That's Florence's obsessed fan. He's always hanging around. Everywhere Florence went, he followed." Eleanor shuddered. "He gives me the creeps. Florence once told me she found him in her garden in Mayfair! He'd learned where she lived and was lurking around, wanting to do who knows what to her."

Dirk tossed aside his napkin. "I'll deal with him. You get these deranged types who can't separate fact from fiction. He knows me, so he won't stick around when I tell him to push off."

"We call him Crazy Charles," Eleanor said.

"Charles?" I asked. "Is that his real name?"

Eleanor nodded. "It wouldn't surprise me if he killed Florence. He pushed himself on her, and she rejected him."

"The man's a menace." Dirk strode away from the table.

"Dirk! Don't startle Charles. I want to speak to him." I hurried after Dirk with Ruby. "There was a fan letter in Florence's bedroom from someone called Charles."

Dirk ignored me. He yanked open the door to the café and lunged at Charles. "Go away! Get out of here, you lunatic."

Charles staggered back, away from Dirk, a startled expression on his face. "I'm doing nothing wrong."

"You're a nuisance. Leave these fine ladies alone. I'll have the police on you if you don't watch yourself."

Charles almost stumbled off the pavement into the road. "I wanted to say how sorry I am. For Florence. You were close to her. I've seen you together."

"You're a damn nuisance. Get out of here." Dirk swatted Charles away as if he was an irritating fly.

"Hold on a moment," I said. "Charles, I'd like to speak to you about Florence."

He froze, and his gaze darted to me, back and forth like his eyeballs were on elastic. "I don't know you. You're not Florence's friend. I know all of her friends. I have pictures of them."

I swiftly made the introductions. "We'd like to know what happened to her."

"He most likely happened to her," Dirk said. "So long as the police don't listen to rumours about me, they'll figure out this one was involved. I should turn him in and do the constabularies job for them. Maybe there's a reward for information. Do you know if there is?"

Charles's mouth dropped open. "I'd never hurt Florence. She was my everything. I adored her."

"Tell that to the coppers," Dirk said. "They won't believe you, and you'll end up behind bars. You're a damn danger, man."

"Let's not make assumptions," I said hurriedly, concerned about the panicked look on Charles's face. "If you could spare us a few minutes, we would like to talk. I heard you were a fan of Florence's work. You must have incredible stories to tell. Perhaps I could buy you a cup of tea."

"Don't talk to him," Dirk said. "He's a lunatic. He'll probably strangle you next."

"Florence wasn't strangled," I muttered under my breath to Dirk. "And you're hardly helping the situation by scaring a potential suspect."

"I make no apologies for assisting ladies in distress," Dirk said. "This man's a killer."

"I didn't do it!" Charles turned on his heel and sped away.

I glared at Dirk, swiftly untied Benji, and we raced after Charles, Ruby hurrying to keep up.

"Dirk may be handsome and make excellent films, but he's a blundering idiot," Ruby said. "All he was worried about was his reputation and the deal falling through. He doesn't give two hoots about what happened to Florence."

"The man we're chasing does," I said as we continued to pursue Charles along the busy London street. "Did you see how red his eyes were? It looks like he's been crying."

"I did. Dirk was quick enough to point the finger at Charles as the killer." Ruby dodged around startled walkers who objected to our unladylike speed. "Looking to deflect attention because he did it, perhaps?"

"Dirk was full of his own self-importance." Charles was getting away from us, and Ruby was wheezing. "Benji, fetch!" I unleashed Benji and watched him fly. My brilliant dog could do anything—hunt a lost piece of sausage, sniff for clues, and bring down fleeing suspects in a murder investigation.

We slowed to a more respectable speed-walk as Benji went to work. He artfully dodged around people, gaining on Charles with every paw step. Charles looked over his shoulder and yelped when he realised Benji was in pursuit. But he was going as fast as he could, and would never outrun my marvellous dog.

Ruby hurried along beside me, one hand pressed against her side. "We should never eat and run. I have a dreadful stitch."

"You'll recover. And lunch was useful. Eleanor is obsessed with getting her name in lights in whatever distasteful way she can manage, and Dirk wanted Florence, her contacts, and her money to make his films."

"Which gives us two new suspects!" Ruby said. "Eleanor wanted what Florence had and needed her out of the way to get it."

I nodded. "And Dirk's deal with Florence was going wrong, and he needed her signature on that paperwork before she changed her mind and he lost everything."

"I don't suppose your friendly police inspector would confirm whether the contract had been signed?" Ruby slid me a sly smile. "After all, everyone can see the way he looks at you."

"Enough of that. I have a love-hate relationship with Inspector Templeton. He hates me for interfering in his business, and I love proving him wrong."

Ruby tittered. "It is such fun to watch you bicker like an old married couple."

I waved away her comment. I planned to grow old in the most disgraceful manner I could achieve, but I'd never marry. "Look! Benji almost has him."

Benji lunged and grabbed the oversized bag Charles had strapped across his body. Charles lost his balance and almost hit the ground. At the last second, he recovered, slipped the bag over his arms, and dodged across the busy street, almost getting hit by an open-topped bus.

"Benji, stop!" I wouldn't risk my precious dog on the roads. The way some people drove was entirely irresponsible.

Benji froze, remaining in flight mode, the bag held between his teeth and his nose pointed in the direction Charles had fled.

We swiftly reached him. I gave him a thorough petting and told him what an excellent boy he was several times before digging out a treat from my pocket and feeding it to him.

"I can't see Charles." Ruby peered across the road as traffic zoomed past. "He must have gone into the park. We'll never find him in there."

"He only ran because of Dirk's idiocy," I said. "Charles is a valuable connection to Florence. If he was such a devoted fan, he could have seen everything she did. He could even have been at the Winter Garden Theatre for her last performance."

Ruby massaged her side. "I need a sit down and a strong cup of tea after that. I was not made for running. My talents lie in lounging and having expensive jewels purchased for me."

I gently extracted the bag from Benji's mouth, and we turned back towards the café. "Let's rejoin Eleanor and Dirk. They may have more information about Charles."

We slow-walked back to the café, taking our time to catch our breath. When we got inside, Benji remaining outside again, Eleanor and Dirk had gone, leaving us with a large bill to pay.

Ruby dropped into her seat, looking unimpressed. "I never trust a man who doesn't pay his own way."

"I agreed to treat Eleanor to lunch, but it was cheeky to assume we'd pay for Dirk, too." I gestured to the waitress and ordered two cups of tea and two treacle tarts with custard.

"Let's see what gifts Benji caught for us, shall we?" Ruby nodded at the bag.

Charles's bag was a plain brown satchel style with a long strap he'd had looped across his body. I opened it, removed empty brown paper bags that must have contained food and looked through a small pile of papers, extracting them so Ruby could see.

"This is your classic stalker compendium," Ruby said after a moment of study. "Look at these pictures of Florence. And half-written letters to her. He really was obsessed. In this one, he's talking about his undying devotion."

"He was a committed fan." I read through a list of Florence's theatre productions, and each one had a tick by them, suggesting he'd either attended the performance or been to the theatre and waited for Florence to arrive and leave so he could catch a glimpse of her.

I pulled out a small wallet and looked through it. I extracted Charles's driver's licence. "Charles Walter Page. Forty-three Henfield Place, London. That'll come in handy."

Ruby flicked through more photographs. "There's a signed one in here. Florence must have met him."

"I wonder how well they knew each other?" I pondered. "He's younger than Florence, but if he'd become a fan in his early twenties, he could have been following her for almost twenty years. Some stars get to know their dedicated fans. They reward them with pictures or lunch dates. Maybe they were friendly."

"Or he was a creepy obsessive," Ruby suggested. "He may have waited at the back entrances of theatres, hoping to grab an unwanted kiss, or hidden at the end of performances and attempted to gain entrance to her dressing room. There may have been nothing benevolent about his relationship with Florence."

"Eleanor was unsettled by Charles's appearance," I said. "Maybe he was a problem."

"Some fans follow their favourite stars everywhere," Ruby said. "He could have been to the Winter Garden Theatre dozens of times, so would have known exactly where to hide. He could have been in the theatre after everyone left the party."

I gathered the pictures and half-written love notes and placed them back in the bag. We drank our tea and took a few peaceful moments to recover ourselves after the unexpected bout of exercise. The perfectly crisp pastry and rich sugary treacle tart soon restored our energy.

"Charles didn't run because he was guilty of anything," I said. "Dirk was playing the hero and scared him away."

"Maybe he sees Charles as the perfect fall guy," Ruby said. "Dirk is guilty of murder, but no one will look at him when they're focused on an obsessed fan. If Charles can be identified as being at the theatre on the night Florence was murdered, he'll find himself in serious trouble."

"Not if we figure out what happened first," I said.

We finished our tea and tart, and the waitress brought over the final bill.

Ruby opened her handbag and rifled around. "I don't get paid until the end of the week, but I'm sure I've got money in here somewhere. Coins are always falling out of my purse."

"This is on me," I said. Ruby was generous to a fault, but had a weakness for the latest fashion, and her employer didn't pay her well for the work she did. Unfortunately, Ruby's family lost most of their fortune during the war, so she struggled with unexpected bills.

"My treat next time." Ruby snapped her handbag shut. "I won't pay for any film producers, though. The nerve of that man to abandon us. If he'd been a gentleman, he'd have waited to see what happened with Charles."

"It does show a lack of sincerity," I said. "I thought Eleanor would have waited. She was most concerned about Charles appearing outside the café."

"Perhaps it was an act." Ruby smoothed down her skirt. "She saw an opportunity to shift the light of guilt away from her and onto a much more vulnerable subject."

"That's a theory to look into." I was collecting my things when the café door swung open. My stomach dropped, and I let out a gentle sigh. Inspector Templeton stood in the doorway.

We'd been caught red-handed once again.

Chapter 12

"If you're here for lunch, I recommend the crab salad. It was excellent." I was determined to remain calm under Inspector Templeton's steely gaze. I adjusted my handbag over my arm and ensured Charles's wallet was tucked inside, away from prying eyes.

"We had a report about a fight. The café owner mentioned two women and a dog were involved. Imagine where my thoughts went to?" Inspector Templeton gestured to the police officer waiting beside him. "Show these ladies outside and make sure they go nowhere. I need to have a few words with the owner before I question them."

"I must get back to work," Ruby said. "Busy afternoon with the horses."

"The horses will wait. Unless you want to do this at the station."

Ruby made a small noise of indignation, then stomped out of the café. The waiting police officer gestured for me to follow her, and after collecting Charles's satchel, I headed outside and joined Ruby and Benji.

"What nonsense. Calling the police over such a small matter," Ruby muttered. "And the way Inspector Templeton was speaking, he considers us the criminals."

"I wouldn't call it small in regards to the investigation. The effort was worth it, since we discovered an important piece of information. The police may know nothing about the mysterious Charles, yet we almost caught him."

Ruby winced and lifted a foot off the pavement. "I'm not sure my feet will ever be the same after running in heels."

"Then get smaller heels. You can have practical and pretty shoes."

"There's no such thing. Look out. Your Mr Grumpy is coming to tell us off."

"He's not mine, although he is most definitely grumpy."

We stood in silence, watching Inspector Templeton's progress. He spoke to a few diners in the café and then came outside. He paused to speak to the officer waiting close by, who then returned to the café.

"Getting your lunch to go?" I asked. "I suppose you have little time to stop with this case to crack. You must have Detective Chief Inspector Taylor breathing down your neck for a result."

"Sergeant Matthers isn't getting lunch. He's conducting witness follow-up questions." Inspector Templeton stood in front of us, still looking unhappy. "What have you gotten yourselves into this time?"

"A simple matter of a pleasant luncheon with new acquaintances," I said. "It wasn't our fault a murder suspect in the case you're leading on stumbled into view."

Inspector Templeton closed his eyes for a second and breathed through his nose. "Tell me everything."

"We have new information," Ruby said, a note of excitement in her voice. "It could solve your case."

Inspector Templeton sighed. "Let's start at the beginning. Who were you having lunch with?"

"Before you get cross, the lunch date wasn't at our instigation," I said.

"I'm still waiting for a name."

This man was so stubborn headed. "After being rudely kicked out of the Winter Garden Theatre by you, Eleanor Dixie approached us. She wanted to be included in Florence's obituary and asked to meet. We arranged a meeting here."

"What about the man you chased? Was he a part of the lunch party?" Inspector Templeton asked.

"There was a man dining with us, Dirk Donovan," Ruby said. "At first, I thought he was charming. Handsome as a prize stallion, but then he opened his mouth, and the illusion fell apart like an over-baked biscuit. All he was interested in was saving his reputation."

"The film director?"

Ruby nodded. "He made claims about his innocence and that it wasn't his fault he was able to exploit up-and-coming starlets. That's how it always was, according to him, so why change things? Of course, he wouldn't change things, because it meant he wouldn't get pretty young things sitting on his lap and stroking his over-sized and thoroughly undeserved ego."

"I'm confused. You weren't expecting Dirk to join you for lunch?" Inspector Templeton asked.

I shook my head. "It was a surprise, and it was clear he had no interest in assisting with your investigation. He was there to see what he could get. But we gathered useful information."

"About Dirk?"

Ruby checked her watch and gasped. "I'm so late! I really must go. Lady M will have my head if I'm tardy for our appointment to see the Russian blue. Such a magnificent stud. The foals are worth a small fortune."

"Go. Enjoy your time with the horses," I said.

"Stay. You can't bolt while I'm asking questions pertaining to your interference in a murder investigation," Inspector Templeton said. "This is a serious matter. You caused a ruckus in a respectable venue and then chased a man across the streets of London."

"It was barely a ruckus," I said. "And we chased him for three streets at the most. We ran most civilly and bumped into no one. Benji was also on his best behaviour. I can tell you everything that happened. Ruby doesn't need to be here."

Ruby was hopping from foot to foot, as if she desperately needed the powder room. "I really must go. I'm driving, and it'll take me an hour to get to the stables. They're in the middle of nowhere."

"Very well. But I may wish to speak to you again," Inspector Templeton said with an overserved sigh.

Ruby kissed my cheek, petted Benji on the head, then rushed away, waving wildly for a passing taxi.

I smiled as my effervescent friend turned heads as she trotted along. She was a real beauty but was blasé when it came to her effect on the opposite sex, unless they were completely unsuitable for her. If only she had better taste in men. Still, it was to my benefit she hadn't found her Mr Right. I wouldn't know what I'd do without my fearless partner by my side. Staring down Inspector Templeton on my own was never fun.

He had his notebook out and was jotting down a few sentences. "What did you talk about during lunch?"

"Mainly Florence, although Dirk did most of the talking. Ruby was correct that he was insistent his reputation remain pristine. The fact he argued about it so fiercely made me think he had something significant to hide."

"Like murder?"

"I didn't say that, but when this investigation is over, look into his dealings with his clients. I suspect the young ladies he works with may not have pleasant things to say about him."

"Added to the list. What else did you discuss?"

"Dirk said he was going into business with Florence and Eleanor. They were on the verge of signing a deal to make films. It sounded exciting, though they were at loggerheads as to who would be the star. According to Eleanor, Florence wanted the main roles, but they both considered her too old."

Inspector Templeton made more notes. "Did they argue?"

"Nothing was said about an argument." I tilted my head. "May I enquire about the paperwork we discovered in Florence's room at the Fireside Inn? From my brief inspection, it was a contract of some sort, is that right?"

He tapped his pencil on his pad. "You could be onto something. There were several pieces of business documentation in that room."

My eyebrows shot up, surprised by him sharing information. "Was it signed? Dirk believes if the contract was signed, he'd have access to Florence's funds. I urged caution, but he believed they had a business, regardless of her no longer being alive."

Inspector Templeton gestured to the police officer, who was still interviewing people inside the café, then turned away. "Walk with me."

I caught hold of Benji's lead, and he walked calmly in between us, stopping only occasionally to sniff an interesting scent on the ground or smell Inspector Templeton's trousers.

"Where are we going?" I asked.

"Show me the route you chased the other man. There was another man, wasn't there? Or did you chase a highly respected film director for some unknown reason?"

"There was. Charles Page." I gestured in the direction we'd pursued Charles. "The respectable film director scarpered without paying the lunch bill. A luncheon he wasn't even invited to. The more I learn about Dirk Donovan, the less respectable he becomes."

"Do you consider him a suspect?"

I hesitated. "I am suspicious of Dirk and Eleanor, but they left the Winter Garden Theatre around the same time as everyone else. If they were seen leaving, it would have been hard for them to sneak back in and assault Florence."

"Where did this other man come from?" Inspector Templeton asked. "Another uninvited guest?"

"While we were talking, Eleanor became agitated. She pointed out a man outside the café and said he was Florence's stalker."

He glanced at me. "I wasn't aware Florence had a stalker."

"According to Eleanor, Charles has been following Florence's career for years. I'd put him in his early forties, so he could have been tracking her career for two decades. Maybe more if he started very young." I looked down at the satchel I carried. "This belongs to him. When we gave chase, Benji captured his satchel."

Inspector Templeton took the satchel I passed to him. He scratched Benji's head. "Good boy. Perhaps we should get you to join the police. You're effective at catching criminals."

"He's good at doing everything. I have a genius dog."

Inspector Templeton nodded as he flipped open the satchel and inspected the contents. "I'm assuming you've had a nose through this?"

"I wanted to see who we were dealing with." I made no apologies for being thorough. "Ruby described the contents as classic stalker fare, and I'm inclined to believe her. There are pictures of Florence. Details of her performances. There are even ticks marked by all the shows. I was wondering if those were performances Charles had been to. He must spend a fortune on tickets. What does he do for work? Maybe he doesn't work. He could have dedicated his life to following Florence, but he'd need an income. An inheritance, perhaps? Or he's a criminal and steals to earn money to stalk Florence."

"Enough with the speculation, Veronica," Inspector Templeton said. "For all you know, you could have been chasing an innocent man. Charles has every right to report you. And Benji could be in trouble if he bit him."

"Benji never bites unless I tell him to. This way." I directed Inspector Templeton towards the park. "I assure you, we had everything under control."

"From the accounts of other diners, that's untrue. You confronted Charles outside the café, and whatever you said made him flee."

"That was Dirk's doing. The man is an imbecile. He lunged at Charles, frightening him. He would never have run otherwise. I wanted to ask him what he knew about Florence. He was such an ardent fan, so he'd have knowledge of her movements. Perhaps he was at the Winter Garden Theatre the night she died and saw the killer go inside."

"Or he crept inside," Inspector Templeton said. "Obsessed fans can become dangerous. I've met a few on previous cases, and they lose themselves in a fantasy world where they believe they have a close relationship with a star."

I repressed a smile, although it was a struggle. "Your statement suggests the information we gathered is useful to your investigation."

Inspector Templeton flipped the satchel closed and placed the strap over his shoulder. "Now and again, you can be useful. You must need to return to work. I'll walk you."

"I'm not a dog! I don't need walking."

"Why do you have to make this so difficult?"

"What am I making difficult?"

"Very well. Allow me to accompany you back to your place of work. I've been sitting at my desk all morning, so the exercise will do me good. I'm being purely selfish. Happy now?"

I lifted my chin. "That's more like it. You're welcome to accompany me and Benji."

We walked in a reasonably companionable silence for a few moments. The flurry of London life passed us by, people entering a bookstore, stopping to browse the latest fashions in the clothing store, or grabbing lunch with friends. London never seemed to sleep.

"How is Florence's obituary coming along?" Inspector Templeton asked.

"Slowly, since someone keeps removing me from venues every time I speak to people connected to her. But I've made progress. This afternoon, I'll be on the telephone talking to her friends. I can't get into trouble doing that, can I?"

"Focus on the job at hand. That is all I ask of you."

We stopped by the entrance to the newspaper offices, and I turned to Inspector Templeton. He appeared to have something on his mind, but had trouble looking me in the eye.

"Is something wrong? Are you feeling lightheaded because you didn't eat any lunch? You should go back to the café," I said. "Or we have a tin of biscuits in the office. Do you like digestives?"

"Perhaps I will get something to eat. Stay out of trouble, Veronica. I have enough problems without looking after you, too." He turned and strode away.

I stood with Benji for a moment and watched him go. Inspector Templeton had an excess of confidence, but he wasn't arrogant. I liked that in a person. He also wasn't unpleasant to look at. He had wonderfully broad shoulders, and I'd always liked my men with dark hair and strong features.

I shook my head. There was no time for that. Inspector Templeton was irksome. The sooner I got Florence's obituary written, the sooner he would be out of my hair.

The rest of the afternoon was spent working on various obituaries, whilst telephoning Florence's family and friends, asking as innocently as I could if she had any enemies. I gathered a few interesting quotes about her fabulous life and acting career, but garnered no joy in discovering anyone who had a grudge against her. Not one harsh enough to want her dead.

The office was soon emptying out, the other reporters and administrative staff calling out cheery goodbyes or shouting to each other to join them at the pub.

I gathered my things, said goodbye to my uncle, and walked into the chilly evening air with Benji beside me. I opened my handbag and looked inside. Charles's wallet sat there. I'd given Inspector Templeton almost everything we'd acquired during the chase, but I wanted to see for myself exactly what Charles was made of.

And now was the opportunity to visit Florence's most devoted fan.

Chapter 13

I'd walked Benji around the same streets for almost an hour, but the cold still seeped into my bones, no matter how briskly we walked.

We had been watching Charles's house, and there was no sign of him. Much to my irritation, there was also no sign of the police showing up to talk to him. I'd left Charles's library card in the bottom of the satchel, so Inspector Templeton knew how to contact him. Perhaps he hadn't discovered the library card.

No, he was confident in his job, even if he was stubborn headed and immensely frustrating, and he wanted this investigation brought to an end as swiftly as I did.

Hurried, light footsteps approached, and I recognised Ruby's rapid pace.

"Sorry I'm late. The horse business took longer than I thought it would, and Lady M wanted the beast ridden several times. She even got in the saddle herself. And he was a beast. He tried to bite me!" Ruby's cheeks were flushed, suggesting she'd spent all afternoon outside undertaking physical activity. She was still in her riding jodhpurs and boots. My mother would be scandalised by her wearing such an outfit in public, but I was used to seeing Ruby in her workwear. It was smart blouses with pleated skirts, or mud-spattered jodhpurs.

"You've missed nothing," I said. "Even Benji is getting tired, and he can walk for hours."

Ruby reached into her handbag and brought out roast beef and mustard sandwiches wrapped in brown paper. She fed a piece of mustard free meat to Benji, before handing me the much-appreciated food. "A gift from Lady M. She thinks I need fattening up."

"Tell her thank you." I spoke around the food in my mouth, forgetting my manners as my hunger took over.

"No police?" Ruby asked.

"No sign of them."

"Perhaps Inspector Templeton visited Charles this afternoon while you were at work."

"I've thought about that. He must have gone back to the café, gathered all relevant information, and then returned to the station to investigate the contents of the satchel," I said. "It's not that late. I've been walking around all this time, and no one has left the building."

"Maybe they won't question Charles until tomorrow," Ruby said.

"Inspector Templeton should keep me informed," I said. "After all, we collected this valuable piece of information for him."

Ruby snickered. "Does he report to you now?"

"No! But it's only polite. We've been helpful. I didn't have to give him the satchel."

"He adores your help," she said, a twinkle of mischief in her eyes. "Has he asked if he can call on you yet?"

"It's not like that."

"I'm not so sure. He looks at you in a certain way. Even Dirk noticed."

"Stop bringing that up. Inspector Templeton looks at me and wishes I'd never been born," I said. "I irritate him, and he irritates me. That is a match not made in heaven."

"I've seen epic films about enemies becoming lovers. It's so romantic." Ruby faked a swoon.

"He is the least romantic man I know. He asked to walk me to the office."

Ruby's laughter grew louder. "Perhaps he'll ask you to trot for him next. Or canter. What a hoot. The poor man is doing his best, but you don't make it easy on him."

"There's nothing to be easy about. I'm not looking for a man. I've had my fill of those irascible creatures, and after my experience with you-know-who, I wish to have nothing more to do with them."

Ruby drew breath, no doubt to say more about my lack of romantic associations, when the front door to Charles's home opened and he came out, his collar turned up, and his head down.

I glanced at Ruby, and she nodded. We waited only a few seconds before following Charles into the night, Benji by my side. Charles kept up a fast pace, keeping his head down and his hands tucked into his coat pockets. It was a chilly night, but the way he was walking, stooped and keeping to the shadows, suggested he didn't want anyone to see him.

"If he keeps going this way, we'll end up at the Winter Garden," Ruby said.

Sure enough, twenty minutes later and after consuming all the sandwiches Ruby had supplied, we were concealed in the shadows watching Charles staring up at the Winter Garden Theatre. The building's lights were on, but the main doors were closed, suggesting there was no performance that evening.

"What's he doing?" Ruby asked.

"I think he's crying," I said. Charles was dabbing his face, a white handkerchief gripped in between his fingers.

"Crying because he's feeling guilty about killing Florence?"

"Or sad because she's gone," I said. "Let's talk to him. With no one else around, we'll seem less intimidating."

"I'm not so sure we will. Go easy on him. He seems fragile."

I arched a brow. "You want me to go easy on a potential killer?"

"Yes! I don't want us to become his next victims."

"He could attempt such an ill-advised action, but he would fail."

"I'm happy to restrain him if he turns nasty." Ruby adjusted the waistband of her jodhpurs. "But I don't want to get blood on my work clothes. It's so hard to get out, and I won't be able to afford another pair of jodhpur's until next month."

"Let's see what he has to say before we resort to fisticuffs and blood being spilled." We emerged from the shadows and were almost upon Charles before he realised he wasn't alone. He startled, then recognition flashed in his eyes. "You! You stole my bag."

"That was Benji, my dog," I said. "And you're fortunate he didn't grab hold of anything else valuable you own."

Charles's eyes were still red, his hair dishevelled, and exhaustion sat beneath his eyes. "Is that bully with you?"

"Dirk? No, we're not friends," I said.

"You weren't friends with Florence, either," Charles said. "I'd know you if you were. I know all her friends."

"How about we start this again?" I suggested gently. "I'm Veronica Vale, and this is Ruby Smythe. We didn't know Florence well, although we've seen several of her performances. I'm in charge of writing her obituary for the London Times. That's what I wanted to talk to you about."

He blinked rapidly several times. "I thought you were another one of them."

"Another one of them?" Ruby asked. "What do you mean?"

"Florence was incredible. She was talented, beautiful, resourceful, and she was rich. Everyone who came into her life wanted something from her. Her time, her money, her contacts. They never just wanted her for who she really was."

"We want none of that," I continued. "But I want to do Florence proud by writing her an incredible obituary. I believe you knew her well, so perhaps you can help."

"I loved her," Charles said. "I only wanted the best for her."

"Shall we take this somewhere warmer?" I asked as an involuntary shudder overtook me. "Florence was staying in the Fireside Inn. You might find comfort by visiting."

He nodded enthusiastically. "I know it well! Whenever Florence performed at the Winter Garden Theatre, she stayed there."

"She did! And perhaps you noticed the owner's name above the door."

His brow furrowed. "Vale. That's you?"

"My family," I said. "We own a number of pubs and taverns. It was my late father's business. The Fireside Inn is safe and much warmer than standing out here grieving."

"I plan to visit all of Florence's favourite places. I would like to go there," Charles said.

I gestured along the street. "Shall we?"

He nodded and turned towards the Fireside Inn. I was careful to situate myself on his left, while Ruby moved to stand on his right side. Benji walked behind us, effectively blocking Charles in and making it harder for him to run. He didn't seem to notice our manoeuvring, so lost in his sadness.

I didn't attempt conversation until we were in the warm, welcoming glow of the pub. Reggie had the fire roaring, and he gave us a cheery wave before gesturing to empty seats close to the fireplace. Once we'd gotten our drinks, it was time to begin the questioning.

"You said you loved Florence," I said to Charles. "It sounds like you were a devoted fan."

"Well, yes. More than that. It's not so simple. I..." Charles looked into the half pint of ale I'd brought him.

"Did you have more than a friendship?"

"We had a bond. It was special. When she could, she made time for me. Florence was good to the people who mattered to her."

Ruby exchanged a disbelieving glance with me. "If Florence gave her energy to all of her fans, she'd never have found the time to step on the stage again."

Charles thumped down his glass. "She cared for me. I know she did. I was special to her."

I gestured for Ruby to tread cautiously, since Charles had a temper. "Did you see her performance at the Winter Garden Theatre?"

He drank deeply from his glass. "I did. She was wonderful. But then she always gave the most incredible performances. Florence was meant for the stage."

"You stayed for the whole show?" Ruby asked.

"Of course. I'd never leave mid-performance. I stayed to the end and was one of the last still clapping. I hoped she'd give an encore, but she didn't come back."

"What did you do after the show?" I asked.

He shrugged. "I walked home."

"Did you go to the performance with anyone?"

Charles shook his head. "My friends get bored with me talking about Florence. They're not into the theatre. I headed home and stayed there. I live in lodgings with Mrs Beamish and three other tenants. She's a good sort, but insists on quiet after eight o'clock. I didn't get back until gone nine, so I had to sneak in and not make a sound."

That was disappointing information. Charles went to the performance alone, purportedly left at the end, and then snuck into his lodgings as quietly as a mouse so no one would hear him. That didn't give him a strong alibi. Certainly not an alibi anyone could verify.

"Is it true what they're saying?" Charles's eyes glinted with tears.

I sipped from my drink. "What are they saying?"

"Someone killed Florence."

"Where did you hear that?"

He withdrew a crumpled news cutting from his pocket and placed it on the table. "There was a piece in the paper. No details confirmed by the police, but I know this is about Florence. I could tell by the description."

"You'll most likely read the full story in tomorrow's paper," I said. "It's true. Florence was killed at the Winter Garden Theatre."

Charles ducked his head, and his shoulders shook.

We gave him a moment with his grief, sipping our drinks and enjoying the warmth of the fire as the gentle chatter from other drinkers drifted around us.

"I know who did it." Charles looked up, his cheeks damp with tears and his nose running. "That snake charmer boyfriend."

"You mean her husband?" I asked. "Hank?"

"The fellow you were having lunch with. Dirk."

Ruby inhaled sharply. "Florence and Dirk had an intimate relationship?"

Charles nodded vehemently. "I was Florence's biggest fan, never missed a show. I even saw her perform abroad. I'm not one of those obsessed types, but I liked to watch her even when she didn't perform, and I know all the places she stayed. I visited her main London home in Mayfair, came here when she performed at the Winter Garden, and I even went up to her country house in Norfolk. I know everything about her."

"And you saw her with Dirk?" I asked. "They were together?"

"Yes. He didn't treat her like she deserved to be treated," Charles said. "Dirk used his good looks to exploit her. If that faker respected her, he wouldn't have been seeing other women at the same time. He should have been devoted to Florence."

Ruby gently cleared her throat. "Florence was a married woman. Perhaps she shouldn't have been seeing anyone else, too."

Charles waved away her comment. "Florence wouldn't have been fooling around behind her husband's back if it weren't for Dirk charming her. Everyone who saw Florence perform believed she was a strong, vibrant woman. But I know everything about her, from her beginnings to how she rose to fame. She was vulnerable and naïve, and men were always taking advantage of her."

"We are aware of Florence's upbringing," I said. "But she was an astute businesswoman."

"Sometimes, a handsome face turns heads and encourages foolish decisions," Ruby said. "I've had the misfortune to experience it myself."

"That's what happened with Florence!" Charles jabbed a finger at Ruby. "And Dirk hated her. When he thought no one was watching, he'd glare at her. Once, I even saw him put something in her drink."

My eyes widened. "Dirk tried to poison Florence?"

"Gosh!" Ruby set down her drink and pushed it away. "What did he give her?"

"It wasn't poison. I'm not sure what it was. Maybe a sedative. I wanted to help, but she was under his influence. Horrible man. If anyone wanted to do something bad to Florence, it was him." Charles's cheeks were pink from the warmth of the fire and his passion. "And I know Dirk was at the Winter Garden Theatre that night. I saw him in the audience."

"Dirk is of interest to the police," I said. "If anything untoward happened between them, they'll figure it out."

"He deserves everything that's coming to him. He's a nasty, grasping rogue."

"Have you been spoken to?" I asked Charles.

He looked momentarily confused. "Who wants to speak to me?"

"The police," I said. "It sounds like you knew everything about Florence's life, so you could have seen something of note at the theatre the night she died. You can help solve the crime."

Charles finished his ale, stood, and wiped his hand across the back of his mouth. "I don't like the police. They think I'm odd. They don't understand me."

"Have you had dealings with them?" Ruby asked. "Gotten into bother?"

"They don't understand what it's like to be a true fan. They've moved me on when I've been waiting for Florence. I need to go." Charles hurried away from the table.

We leapt up and rushed after him.

"Wait a moment, we have more questions," I said. "We need to know more about Florence."

Charles pulled open the door and hurried out without looking back.

"Talk of the police got him spooked," Ruby murmured.

"We're not letting him go again." I dashed into the cold air and was dazzled by the flash of a camera bulb. The light was so intense I was temporarily blinded and could only see a bright circle of white. From Ruby's cry of protest, she had experienced the same indignity.

"Well, well. What's Veronica Vale doing chasing after a strange man?"

Chapter 14

I rubbed my eyes, hoping the sharp female voice I'd heard was a walking nightmare. Unfortunately, when my vision cleared sufficiently, Isabella Michaels stood in front of me carrying an unwieldy-looking camera, a smirk on her face, and a notepad sticking out of her oversized jacket pocket.

"Cat got your tongue?" she asked when I didn't respond. "Or are you figuring out a convenient lie?" Her gaze went to Charles, who looked just as stunned by having his photograph taken. "Hello, Charles."

He blinked several times. "You're that gossipy reporter."

"How do you know each other?" I asked.

"I go to the best parties and get the best stories." Isabella tucked an errant strand of dark hair behind one ear. "And dear Charles is always lurking around the famous types."

"You must have to sneak into those parties. You wouldn't receive an invitation," Ruby said.

Isabella rolled her eyes. "Interesting fashion choice you're wearing. Your latest beau must be losing interest if he's not dressing you in the latest styles. Or any style. And you smell like manure."

Ruby's cheeks flamed, and only my hand on her arm stopped her thumping Isabella.

"How's the scandal sheet treating you?" I asked.

"We're getting by nicely on all the local scandal," Isabella said. "Distribution numbers are up. Shame the same can't be said for the London Drudge. Such a stuffy newspaper."

"You must be desperate for content if you're hanging around a respectable venue like the Fireside Inn, stirring up trouble."

She snorted her derision, but I didn't miss the flash of anger in her eyes. "It wasn't so many years ago this place was a watering hole for villains and cads. And rumour has it a few members of the London mob whiled away their time here. Have any comment on that? On the record, naturally."

"What happened before my family purchased the inn is none of your concern," I said.

"It's respectable veneer is masking something," Isabella said. "The apple doesn't fall far from the tree."

"If you're referring to my late father, he was a hearty, healthy oak who looked after people."

"I'm sure there was a rotten core in that oak. Like father, like daughter."

I took a step towards her. "Take that back. You're always chasing after my family, but you'll get no dirt on us."

"Is that so?" A glitter of something unpleasant lit her dark gaze. "I've got plenty of dirt. Perhaps you'll see it on the front page one of these days, and my name will be on the byline."

"Only if it's a slow news day," I said. "There's nothing of note in my family's past."

I despised Isabella digging around in my family's background. My father had never hidden his dealings with a few less than savoury types, but his heart was always in the right place. Every building he purchased was renovated and helped to bring an area up. And if he found any member of staff had a criminal record, he gave them the benefit of the doubt and ensured they still had employment. Isabella was only grubbing around because she was jealous I had the position she longed for. A role at a respectable newspaper.

"Have you been to any good funerals lately?" Ruby asked Isabella. "Veronica tells me you like to lurk around the headstones like a macabre ghoul. Looking for a grieving widower to pounce on?"

Isabella scowled at her. "Funerals are ideal places to get information. Mourners have their guards down and want a shoulder to cry on. Far be it for me to deprive them of that."

"It's unseemly," Ruby said.

"Veronica attends the funerals, so I have as much right to be there, too."

"I go because the families invite me after I've written fitting obituaries for the deceased," I said. "I don't skulk around listening to private conversations, hoping to grab gossip and publish it inappropriately."

"I go where the work takes me. Some of us aren't as fortunate as to have an uncle who owns a newspaper," Isabella sniped.

I gritted my teeth, refusing to engage with her bitter tongue for a moment longer. We regularly butted heads when it came to my role at the newspaper and her less than prestigious position as a gossip journalist for the Daily Review.

"Why were you outside the Fireside Inn?" I asked.

"The same reason you were inside. Following a story. And what a story! Florence Sterling murdered in cold blood. I'm determined to get the inside scoop and see my name on the byline of the front page."

"You're more suitable for page six with the gossip snippets and adverts for cigarettes," Ruby said. "It's easy to flick past those."

"I'm glad to hear you read my newspaper."

"I wouldn't waste a penny on it. Veronica, we should leave."

Charles had been edging away the whole time we'd been bickering.

I caught hold of his arm. "Not so fast. We haven't finished our conversation."

"How very dare you, Charles!" Isabella scolded. "Running out on a lady of Veronica's reputation. Mind you, she chases off most of the men who are interested in her. Did you know her fiancé called off their engagement because she was such a cold fish?"

Ruby whacked Isabella's arm. "At least Veronica has been engaged."

"I'd rather remain single than saddle myself with some hapless sop who has no backbone."

Isabella was in full spite mode this evening. First a dig at my career and now my failed relationship. She must be struggling to find a story if she was attempting to get a rise out of me.

I yanked Charles closer, but he tugged his arm away and surprised me with a firm shove. Benji barked as I stumbled.

Charles turned to make a run for it, but Isabella pulled a stick from her large handbag and smacked him on the back of the head with it.

He slumped to his knees and groaned, holding his head. "What did you do that for?"

"I'm the only one who gets to shove Veronica when she's being shrill and irritating," Isabella said. "Stay there until you learn to behave around ladies."

Charles took his hand away from his head. "I'm bleeding! You made me bleed."

"I'll do worse than that if you keep misbehaving." Isabella prodded Charles's shoulder with what I could now see was a short policeman's truncheon.

"Did you steal that?" I asked.

"No! Well, I acquired it by interesting means. A lady has to protect herself on the mean streets of London. Don't you agree?"

"Is Charles badly hurt?" Ruby crouched beside him.

"It does hurt," Charles said.

"It serves you right," Isabella said. "We're not done questioning you."

"You're not involved in this interview," I said.

"So, you are interviewing him about Florence's murder! I knew it."

I glowered at Isabella. "Benji, guard Charles. Give him a nip if he moves."

"I won't move. I don't need a dog bite, too," Charles said.

Benji positioned himself in front of Charles, his stance alert and his gaze fixed on him.

"Which parties did you see Charles at?" I asked Isabella.

"Any gatherings that involved Florence, he was there," Isabella said.

My breath caught in my throat. "Were you at the Winter Garden Theatre the night she died?"

"Naturally. I missed most of the performance, though, since theatre is entirely dull. But I was there when the audience exited, and I accompanied the star and her friends to the official after-show gathering. They may not like me, but they need to remain on my good side for fear I'll publish their scandal and ruin them." Isabella fluttered her lashes. "I was surprised to see you didn't make the guest list. Although your fashion sense is more last century than flapper."

I tugged on the mildly frayed hem of my respectable coat sleeve. "That's when you saw Charles?"

"He was there. Same as always."

"At the actual party?" Ruby asked.

"No. I saw him outside the theatre before the performance began, and then in the foyer afterwards. I take photographs at the beginning and end of each show. Those photographs reveal what the theatregoers actually thought of the performance. If they sat through two and a half hours of dullness, they look tired and their shoulders sag. However, if they were buoyed by the entertainment, they'll be happily chatting."

"How did people seem after Florence's performance?"

"They enjoyed it. Most of them, anyway. I adore doing pieces on puffed-up celebrities who think they are the bee's knees, but the reality hits home when they see the sad-faced, miserable people leaving their shows." Isabella gave an impish grin. "The number of gift baskets and pleas to change my story that arrive when I publish one of those pieces is hilarious. I'm always being sent things to bribe me."

"The joys of working on a gossip rag," Ruby said.

Isabella lifted one shoulder. "It's only temporary."

I bit my tongue. I was around the same age as Isabella, and we'd started in the industry after the war. Ever since she began publishing puff pieces on celebrities, she'd been saying it was temporary until she got her foot in the door of a respectable newspaper. Initially, I'd had sympathy for her, but when she badmouthed me and started showing up uninvited to funerals, my tolerance level for Isabella Michaels decreased to nothing.

However, as infuriating as I found her, she had an excellent nose for a story. "If I tell you what I was doing in the Fireside Inn with Charles, will you share what you saw at the party?"

"On the record?"

I shook my head. "This must be unofficial. I'm writing Florence's obituary, but I'm also looking into what happened to her."

Isabella glanced at Charles. "I know she was killed."

"I'll tell you what I know, but you must do the same."

Ruby said, "We can't trust her. She'll publish everything you tell her."

"On my reporter's oath, I won't." Isabella shook her head. "Florence Sterling wasn't my cup of tea, but no old girl deserves to be snuffed out like that. It's not on."

"There's no such thing as a reporter's oath, but we could be useful to each other," I said. And I was more than a little keen to get an insider view about what happened at that party.

"In this instance, I agree," Isabella said.

I glanced at Ruby as she stood from her inspection of Charles's head wound. "How bad?"

"Just a kiss. He'll be fine."

"I don't feel fine. I want to go home." Charles went to stand, but a growl from Benji kept him on his knees.

"So, the party?" I prompted Isabella.

"It was your usual thing. Overdressed celebrities wearing too much make-up and perfume, twittering around each other. Everyone fawned over Florence, and she took it in her usual amenable way. I liked her. Often there's not much substance to celebrities when you meet them when the glitz and glamour slides away, but she had gumption." Isabella flashed up her eyebrows. "Now you."

"Florence had a connection to my family," I said. "She stayed at the Fireside Inn when she performed at the theatre. I met her a few times when I was younger, and I agree with your character assessment."

"I remember reading that she patronised local businesses. Something about not forgetting her roots." Isabella's gaze flicked to the inn. "It makes sense she'd stay somewhere so working class."

I ignored the jibe. "What else happened at the party? Did you see Charles attempting to get in?"

"I didn't," Charles said. "And I've already told you I attended the performance."

"This sad little creature was always trailing after Florence. I took pity on him one freezing night and brought him out a thermos of tea for fear he'd freeze to death," Isabella said.

"Charles may have snuck inside," Ruby said. "Then he waited for everyone to leave."

"There was security at the venue, so it would have been impossible for an outsider to get in. If your name wasn't on the exclusive guest list, you wouldn't get an opportunity to rub shoulders with Florence." Isabella half smiled.

"If no one snuck in, it must have been someone close to Florence who killed her," I said.

Isabella nodded. "That makes sense."

"It was Dirk!" Charles said. "You can't trust him."

"Dirk Donovan?" Isabella tilted her head and her brow furrowed. "He flirted with me at the party."

"Gosh! I find that unlikely," Ruby said. "Are you remembering the right party? You have a weakness for bubbles."

"I go to several parties every week, and I remember every detail. Dirk was there, and he complimented me on my new hairstyle." She patted her fashionable short bob.

"Did you see Dirk have a problem with Florence?" I asked. "Perhaps they argued."

Her smile sharpened. "I should say I did. Dirk took her to one side when he thought no one could see them, and they had a heated debate."

"What was it about?"

"I couldn't get close enough to hear most of the conversation, but I heard a few words. It sounded like Dirk wanted money, or they were involved in a deal, but Florence wanted to pull out."

"They planned on setting up a production company," I said. "Florence, Dirk, and Eleanor Dixie were going into the film business together."

"From what I saw, that deal had gone sour," Isabella said. "Dirk was furious when Florence brushed him off and returned to her guests."

I turned to Ruby. "Florence would have trusted Dirk. If he'd returned to the theatre after everyone left, she'd have let him in."

"Oh, this is delightful." Isabella rocked back on her short heels and grinned. "I know something the incredible Veronica Vale doesn't. It feels good to get one up on you."

"It wasn't Dirk who returned to the theatre?" I turned back to her. "What did you see?"

"I wish I hadn't agreed to share now," Isabella said.

"Don't keep secrets," Ruby said. "We have an unsolved murder on our hands, and we need to ensure the right person goes down for the crime. Tell us what you know."

Isabella pursed her lips. "If I tell you, I want exclusive photographs."

"Photographs of what?" I asked.

"Of the place Florence Sterling was actually murdered."

"And where would that be, if it wasn't the Winter Garden Theatre?"

Her gaze flicked to the Fireside Inn. "Right here."

Chapter 15

Despite the delicious smell of grilled bacon and fresh, warm bread, I had little appetite the following morning as I sat on the end of my mother's bed with Matthew, Benji by my feet eagerly awaiting treats. I'd barely slept the previous night, thinking about everything Isabella had told us.

"Get some breakfast inside you," my mother said. "It sounds like you have a busy day ahead of you."

I'd been updating them about the latest discoveries in Florence Sterling's murder. Despite going over it time and again in my head and talking it through with them, Isabella's revelation still astonished me.

"Isabella lied to you," Matthew said. "Florence didn't die at the Fireside Inn."

"She sounded credible," I said. "Isabella was at the party with everyone, and when it finished around ten thirty, the partygoers headed home. Just after eleven-thirty, Isabella saw Florence come out of the Winter Garden Theatre and return to the inn."

"If she didn't die at the theatre, why was her body found there?" my mother asked. "It makes no sense. A corpse doesn't get up and walk about on its own."

"That's what I need to figure out," I said. "Florence must have been killed in her room at the inn and moved to the theatre to confuse the investigation."

"It's working," my mother said. "I don't know if I'm coming or going. Veronica, are you being safe? I don't like you lurking around dark and dangerous streets in the dead of night investigating a crime. It's not becoming for a young lady."

"Mother, I'm hardly young, and I wasn't lurking. Well, perhaps I was, but I was doing so with Ruby and Benji. Isabella should have been the one who was worried. She was on the streets alone, gossip stirring."

"It must have been that chap you told us about," my mother said. "The one who watched Florence."

"Charles Page," I said. "He could be involved. Isabella said she watched him follow the car after it left the theatre with Florence in it. He knew where Florence stayed every time she performed at the Winter Garden Theatre, so it would have been a simple enough task to tail her."

"Then he snuck inside the inn, somehow got to Florence's room, and murdered her?" Matthew appeared puzzled. "Reggie would never allow that."

I shook my head. "I know. That's a problem. Reggie's got a sharp eye. He would have heard a fight and investigated."

"The performance was on a Sunday night," Matthew said. "It's busy at the inn on the weekends."

"How would you know? You haven't left this house for over a month," my mother said. "And it shows. I don't like how pale your skin is. You need exercise and fresh air. Well, as fresh as the air is in this city."

"I get plenty of exercise in the garden," Matthew said. "I'm always out there looking after the animals."

"That's not enough!" She flipped back the covers to reveal Quillon and Peregrine snuggled against her side. "The pugs need more than a brisk walk around the garden."

I smiled indulgently. The two pugs seemed most content. They barely left my mother's bed, other than for brief toilet duties and a sniff of air in the garden with Matthew.

"Don't get attached," I said. "The dogs' home will find them somewhere permanent soon."

"Good riddance to them when they do," my mother said. "My allergies plague me when we have anything furry in the house."

I shared an amused look with Matthew, and was tempted to ask if she'd forgotten about the long-term foster cats who were always trotting around, Benji, who was a permanent resident, and the two kittens Matthew was hand-rearing.

"You'll miss them when they're gone," I said.

"I'll be glad to have the bed to myself." My mother's tone was light, but I noticed a touch of sadness in her eyes. She never admitted to feeling lonely since my father's death, but I knew the truth.

"Don't waste your time listening to anything Isabella has to tell you," Matthew said. "She can't be relied upon."

I busied myself with my cup of tea. Matthew was biased when it came to Isabella. They'd dated not long after Matthew returned home from the war. Things had gone well, but he developed a worrying health problem that had yet to be diagnosed. Symptoms included memory loss, an inability to talk when stressed, and sometimes trouble moving. The doctor could find no reason for his illness, but his condition flared up when he'd courted Isabella, and she'd abandoned him. She was a sore spot in his life, one he was yet to move past.

"For all you know, Isabella followed Florence to the inn, desperate to get a scoop. She figured Charles would try to do something to Florence, but when he didn't, she acted," Matthew said.

"Goodness me!" my mother exclaimed. "Such a dainty little thing is no killer."

"She's sneaky and small," Matthew said. "It would have been easy for her to creep into the inn. She got up to the guest rooms, found Florence, and attacked her."

I considered this possibility and dismissed it as outlandish. "How would a woman of such small stature have moved the body back to the theatre? She would have left a trail of clues."

"That's for you to figure out," Matthew said. "You're the expert on death. Providing she could get the body down the stairs, she could have shoved Florence into a car and sped back to the theatre. She must know the back ways into the theatre. She's so secretive and snoopy."

"I'll add the theory to our list of possibilities," I said.

"Leave this murder business alone," my mother said. "You've told us the police have details of the stalker. Once they've spoken to him, he'll confess, and this will be over. It's unnatural for you to lurk and watch criminals."

"What if it's not Charles?" I asked. "What if there's more to the story?"

"Let the police do their job and stop poking your nose where it doesn't belong. You're meddling in matters that aren't your concern."

I sighed, knowing my mother's words held truth, but I couldn't shake the feeling something about this case was amiss, and I was determined to uncover it.

"I do need to focus on finishing Florence's obituary," I said. "Perhaps you're right. Charles did seem unstable, and he became nervous when we spoke about the police. Isabella said he followed Florence around like a lost puppy."

"Puppies sometimes bite," Matthew said.

"Ignore your brother. He's being mawkish. Give Florence a proper sendoff in her obituary. And make sure you mention her pugs. I expect she's looking down on them, wanting to know they're happy." Mother gently stroked each pug, and they gave soft grunts of contentment. "Mind you, they must be feeling like they've moved down a notch in society since lodging here. Did you see all the toys you brought back for these creatures?"

"The box was heavy, but I haven't looked at any of them," I said.

"I'm sure the collars were tailormade. But it's no wonder the dogs don't want to wear them. They're heavy. They must make their necks sore. Not that they have much in the way of a neck. Stubby little things."

I eyed Quillon, who now had his head nestled on my mother's pillow. "They don't seem to mind their current situation. Our home is hardly a hovel."

"Matthew, finish your breakfast, then I insist you take the dogs for a proper walk. No more of this garden meandering." Mother leaned forward in her bed. "And when was the last time you brushed your hair?"

Matthew dodged her curious hand as she tried to smooth his messy curls. "They don't like walking far. I do three laps of the garden with them, and then I have to pick them up and bring them in. They refuse to walk. If I take them out on the streets, they'd be terrified." His gaze shifted to the window, and he licked his lips.

"Florence used to walk them," I said. "And although it's cold, the sun is out."

He slid off the bed, taking his plate with him. "Another time. I've got things to do."

"What things?" my mother called after him. "There's a list of shopping I need you to get."

"Veronica can do that," Matthew called out. A door shut, bringing an end to the conversation.

My mother heaved a sigh. "I don't know what to do with that boy. Every day is a struggle for him."

"Matthew has good and bad days," I said. "Perhaps we could get the doctor to speak to him the next time he visits you. Just to make sure there's nothing concerning him."

Her eyes hazed with tears. "Sometimes, he won't speak to me."

"It's not because he's angry with you." I'd been reading reports of soldiers back from the war who struggled to readjust. Matthew had been on the front line and must have seen terrible sights. I sometimes heard him calling out in his sleep, experiencing nightmares, but he never talked about them and claimed he didn't remember his dreams. But his subconscious did, and those days serving his country haunted him.

"It's a pity things didn't work with Isabella," my mother said. "She was so charming when she called here."

"Isabella is wrong for Matthew," I said firmly. "She's too focused on her career to give him enough attention."

"There's truth in that statement. Being too career-minded isn't the behaviour of a polite young lady." My mother fixed me with an unblinking stare. "I should ask my friends if they have suitable daughters or nieces. There's a shortage of eligible bachelors since the war. There must be someone appropriate for Matthew and his ... needs. A gentle girl. Not too ambitious."

"Why don't you let Matthew make his own decisions when it comes to his romantic affairs?"

She sighed again. "I must intervene. The boy never leaves the house! His bride won't appear on the doorstep seeking him out. You are both lost causes. I shall never have grandchildren."

"Why do you need grandchildren when you have fur babies?" We'd had this debate many times. If I conceived a child at my age, I'd be considered a geriatric mother, which wasn't appealing. And although I didn't find babies disagreeable, I preferred to cuddle a kitten than an infant.

"I get a small amount of comfort from the waifs and strays you bring home," my mother said, "but nothing smells nicer than a baby."

"Even when its nappy is full?" I shook my head as I grimaced. "Benji's freshly washed fur is a delight. You should wash those pugs. They'd fit in the kitchen sink."

"I don't have the strength to lift them, let alone the energy to wash them!"

"Which is why you have a strapping son living at home to do that for you." I stood and gathered our plates and cups. "I need to leave for work. Keep an eye on Matthew. When he goes into himself, I worry about him."

"He shreds my nerves with his dark moods." My mother smoothed her covers. "I will get to work on finding him a suitable lady friend. We need more laughter in this house. Your father always made things brighter."

I kissed my mother's cheek. "You both made this house a wonderful place to grow up in."

She patted the back of my hand. "We had fun, didn't we?"

I looked around the cluttered bedroom, full of dusty photographs and knickknacks gathered from my father's adventures as he sought new places to buy and renovate. There were so many memories within these walls. If I was in my mother's situation, I'd pack it away, donate it, or sell it, and move somewhere new. But I understood living somewhere for decades meant your roots went deep, and the thought of slicing through those roots was too much to deal with.

"Off you go to work," my mother said. "Make me proud. Remember to take a scarf."

After leaving the crockery in the kitchen, knowing Matthew would tidy it away when he emerged from his room, I dashed to the newspaper office with Benji. I had a busy day ahead of me with half a dozen obituaries to write and others to check before submitting for the deadline.

After greeting everyone in the office, I settled at my desk. I had a task to do before I attended to the obituaries. I telephoned Hank, Florence's husband. I wanted final words from him about Florence, and I was planning to ask discreet questions, to see if he'd been aware she'd had an ardent stalker.

Kathleen answered my call, and she made me an appointment for four o'clock that afternoon at Florence's primary residence. Satisfied I was tying up the loose ends for Florence's obituary, I got my head down and dashed out over two thousand words for a respected vicar, a retired nurse, and a science teacher who'd all recently departed this world.

I'd been so immersed in the fascinating lives of the recently dead, I'd lost track of the time, so it was a mad dash out of the office with Benji, calling to my uncle that I'd be back later. I had been so focused on writing that I hadn't stopped for food, and my stomach was grumbling.

I reached for my handbag, where I always kept emergency rations. Drat! In my haste to leave, I'd left it at the office. "No late lunch for us, Benji! Maybe we can squeeze in an afternoon tea if we spot somewhere that permits dogs."

He wagged his tail, not seeming to mind. And he hadn't gone without. There was always a bowl of dog biscuits tucked under my desk.

With a bit of luck, Hank would offer refreshments. It appeared Kathleen was still working for him despite Florence being gone, and she seemed a capable assistant, so at the least, I'd get a decent cup of tea and perhaps a biscuit.

I checked the time, ensured I had a few coins in my pockets, and waved down a taxi, requesting it let us out two streets from our destination, so we could stretch our legs.

We arrived ten minutes early, but I was keen to get the interview completed so I could stop by the police station to see what Inspector Templeton had to say about Charles Page. I hoped he had done nothing rash, like charging him with murder.

"Let's take a lap around the streets, shall we, Benji? Then we'll see if Hank has anything useful for us."

Benji softly woofed his agreement. He was never happier than when on a walk or when he had his head in a bowl of food.

I was approaching Florence's Mayfair residence, where we had planned our meeting, when I slowed. Hank stood at the front door with his arms around Eleanor Dixie, and they were kissing.

Chapter 16

I was so shocked, I barely had the good sense to conceal myself behind a tree as Hank and Eleanor continued their passionate embrace. Anyone passing would be able to tell they were more than friends. It was scandalous. The man had no shame. Florence's funeral hadn't even been arranged, and he was already moving on.

It was not the behaviour of a grieving husband.

I stood with Benji for several minutes until Eleanor pried herself away from Hank. Her light giggle drifted towards me as she hurried in the opposite direction from where I was hidden, turning and waving at Hank several times, as if they were happy young lovers with nothing to hide.

My stride was determined as I marched towards the house with Benji. I had to confront Hank. This affair gave him an ideal motive for wanting Florence dead. Unless the relationship had started within the last seventy-two hours, this had been going on while Florence was alive, and they were clearly comfortable in each other's company as well as in each other's arms.

Hank could have tired of having a more mature wife. Or he resented Florence because she was the star in the relationship and he felt overshadowed. Florence had brought in the bulk of their income, and it would take a man with broad shoulders and an open mind to accept such a situation.

I knocked sharply at the door and was about to knock again when Hank opened it. He checked his watch and smiled. "Right on time."

"Good afternoon. I never like being late for appointments. A person's time is important, and if you leave them waiting, it suggests you think little of them."

Hank grinned. "Good for you. My timekeeping is terrible. Florence used to tease me that she'd set my watch back half an hour, so I'd arrive on time for things."

"That's an excellent idea."

"Please, come in. I'd offer refreshments, but my tea-making ability is a disaster. It always turns out like used dishwater."

My stomach grumbled its unhappiness, but that was the last problem troubling me. "I won't stay long. As I mentioned to Kathleen on the telephone, I wanted to get final words about Florence, so everything is right for her obituary."

"Absolutely. We need to do her proud." Hank collected two wineglasses from the table, one of them with a pink lipstick mark on the rim. He was barely hiding the evidence of his recent liaison.

The room we were in exuded understated elegance and was more refined than the front parlour where I'd had to tease Peregrine out from underneath the chair.

"Doing your own cleaning? Is Hetty not here?" I asked.

"I let her go. She was always complaining about something. Besides, I wanted the place to myself. Take a seat. I won't be a moment."

I perched on the edge of a pink chair with embroidered cushions and waited for Hank to return from the kitchen.

"No Kathleen, either?" I called out.

"She's been in and out all day. Florence had several places she rented or lived in around London. Kathleen's gone to complete inventory at the stucco house in Belgravia to see what can be saved, sold, or stored." Hank returned, sat in the chair opposite me, and crossed his legs. "Florence loved to spend her money on beautiful things. I suppose that's why she married me."

I pressed my lips together and pretended to remove a piece of lint from my skirt.

He clapped his hands together. "What questions do you need to ask me?"

"It would be helpful to know who Florence spent most of her time with," I said. "Those who influenced her, or whom she influenced. I believe she mentored Eleanor Dixie."

If Hank was surprised by Eleanor's name being mentioned, he didn't show it. Perhaps he had better acting skills than I realised. "Florence once said she thought of Eleanor as more like a daughter. She said that if she'd ever had children, she'd have liked them to be like Eleanor. She's smart, pretty, of course, and hard-working. All excellent qualities you need to survive this ruthless business."

"Eleanor must be heartbroken over losing Florence," I said.

"We all are. Her star shone so brightly that the world seems dull now she's gone," Hank said. "Would you like a brandy? It's early, but I find it helps settle the nerves."

"Not for me, thank you. What have you got to be nervous about?"

Hank was already on his feet and walking to the drinks cabinet at the back of the room. "I'm not nervous, but it will take time to get used to not having Florence in my life. She was an extraordinary woman. She wanted everyone to remember her for her talent, not because she died a grisly death alone in her dressing room."

While Hank talked, I peered under the chair he'd been seated in. Something black and silky was tucked underneath it.

I gestured Benji to the chair. "Fetch."

He trotted over and yanked out a black piece of silk.

Hank turned as Benji returned it to me. "What's your dog got?"

I carefully extracted the silky slip from between Benji's teeth and held it between two fingers. "You must forgive Benji. He's most skilled at finding lost things."

Hank's cheeks coloured as he set down the generous glass of brandy he'd poured himself. "That must have belonged to Florence. For all her talents, she never learned the skill of keeping things tidy. Hetty always complained about her mess, even though she was generously paid to clean it up."

"This is from Paris," I said as I inspected the label.

"Like I said, Florence loved to spend. And why not? She earned it." He held out a hand. "I'll put it with her clothes."

I shook my head. "The cut is daring. Something a younger woman would wear, don't you think?"

"I can't say I know much about ladies' undergarments." Hank busied himself with his brandy and wouldn't look me in the eye.

"There is no need to be bashful. From what I understand of your relationship with Florence, it wasn't a traditional marriage."

He slid me a glance. "I hope you're not putting that in her obituary?"

"There will be nothing but good things said about Florence. I have a deep respect for the lady, but I would like to know who this belongs to."

"What's it got to do with you?"

"Perhaps nothing, but Florence's murder is still under investigation."

Hank's eyebrows rose. "And again, that is none of your concern. A tragedy happened, and I'll admit to seeking comfort in a difficult time, but I refuse to be judged because of that."

"I'm not judging, but I am curious about what happened to Florence."

"That's a police matter." Hank sank into his chair, the brandy glass in his hand. He didn't speak, and neither did I.

I let the silence stretch between us, the softly ticking clock on the mantelpiece over the fireplace the only noise breaking the silence.

Hank finally looked up at me, and there was a weariness in his eyes I'd not seen before. "We had an open marriage. It's not something everyone understood, but it suited us. Florence wanted a husband to show off to get the gossip churning. She adored having me on her arm because everybody talked about us."

"It was a marriage of convenience?"

"There was affection there, but little passion. Don't misunderstand me, to begin with, we were a married couple in every sense, but Florence was obsessed with her career. I'd often not see her for weeks when she was touring or working on a new film." Hank sipped from his glass. "Things grew worse when she became interested in making her own films. She forgot me, and noticed other chaps."

"I was aware Florence had entanglements with other men," I said.

"That information had better not go in the obituary, either. It was an open secret within our close circle of friends, but one we didn't share publicly."

"I promise, it won't. The London Times is respectable. I'll ensure everyone remembers Florence fondly. But it's so wrong what happened to her. And I agree with her sentiments about her lasting legacy. She should have gone out in a blaze of starlit glory. Her death was a tragedy."

Hank nodded. "I'd appreciate that. Florence wasn't selfish. She didn't date other men because she cared nothing for me. She was the one who suggested an open marriage when I complained about her working away. At first, I was shocked. But I missed having a companion."

"You didn't resent being a trophy husband rather than a real husband?"

"It took adjustment, and we argued about it now and again. We both agreed any entanglements would remain uncomplicated."

"Does that mean neither of you could fall in love with anyone else?"

"You got it. So long as we kept things casual and fun and returned to each other when we were needed, everything worked."

"Until it didn't?" I pointed at the slip I'd discarded on the chair beside me.

"That's not serious. It's fun. And I'm lonely. I'm also sad my wife is dead."

"The slip belongs to Eleanor, doesn't it?" I asked. "And before you lie, you should know, I always arrive early for my appointments. If you plan on a dalliance so soon after Florence's death, I would advise more caution. Some newspapers adore scandal."

He set down his glass with a thud. "Eleanor is far too young for me. My wife just dead and you accuse me of fooling around with her protégé."

"I always believe my own eyes. And what I witnessed gave me cause to question your character," I said.

Hank lifted his chin. "I have nothing to be ashamed of. I am not being unfaithful with Eleanor. Florence wouldn't have approved of that association. Too close to home."

The fact he couldn't look me in the eye suggested definite shame. I felt a sliver of sympathy for the man. He'd been in an odd marriage, so it was little wonder he struggled.

"This will all be over soon, anyway." Hank appeared to pull himself together and forced a smile. "The police have been in touch and said they have a man in custody."

"So I understand," I said. The topic of infidelity was closed, but Hank had chosen to lie to me, and that made me suspicious of him. "Did you see Florence arguing with anyone at the party after the show? Someone who decided to teach her a lesson that night?"

"No, but we were busy mingling. I suppose she could have disagreed with someone, but I can't imagine anyone at the party would have wished her harm."

"The police didn't tell you who they were questioning?"

"Not a thing. Do you know who he is?"

I slid past his question. "Not one of your romantic entanglements that got complicated?"

"Good gracious! Most certainly not. My lady friends are respectable."

Since I'd weaved past the obituary and into the world of suspects, I grabbed the proverbial bull by the horns. "You had no reason to debate with Florence over anything that night?"

"We were happy! The few times we came together that evening, we exchanged pleasantries and moved on," he said. "Why? Has someone been telling lies about me?"

I shook my head. Hank was the only one being untruthful. "Do you have any final memories of Florence? A lasting image of her? Perhaps from that evening."

Hank thought for a moment, his gaze drifting around the room. "I will remember her tenderly. I suppose my final image was of her in her theatre dressing room. I attempted to convince her to come home, but she had so many ridiculous superstitions and habits to avoid bad luck befalling her performances. I was tired and didn't have the energy to bicker with her."

While Hank reminisced, I sat in silence. He had motive and a weakness for alcohol, a substance that always impaired judgement. He'd also been carrying on an affair with someone Florence wouldn't have approved of. Had she caught him out so he silenced her?

Did the police have the wrong man?

Chapter 17

"Veronica! I need revisions on the vicar's obituary. His widow stopped by half an hour ago with additional information." Uncle Harry's voice rumbled out of his office, where the door was rarely closed.

I'd been sneaking off after dashing back to my desk to collect my handbag when my uncle accosted me. I pivoted on my heel. "Bob will assist. I'm off to the police station for an update on the Florence Sterling case."

"I'm not doing your job for you." Bob marched over, his suit still crumpled at the crotch, suggesting he hadn't moved from his chair for hours. "The dead are your pet project. You love anything ghoulish."

"The death of a loved one is never ghoulish. It's a tragedy that must be respected and appropriately honoured using the number of column inches the family desire to purchase." I inched towards the door. "I really must go."

"This won't wait." My uncle strode out of his office and joined us. "We go to print in thirty minutes. They need the final copy for the dead vicar."

This couldn't be more inconvenient. I'd intended to present Inspector Templeton with the news of Hank and Eleanor's affair. The more I discovered about their situation, the more I was convinced the police had the wrong man and Charles was innocent.

My uncle caught hold of my elbow and tugged me back to my desk. "This won't take long. I knew Reverend Whiting, and he was a good man. And I don't want to cross swords with his widow. Vicars' wives are terrifying. They always appear like such meek souls, but they have fire and brimstone rolling inside them. If she wants a change, we make it. No questions asked."

Bob smirked the whole time my uncle spoke. He rocked back and forth on his heels like a grubby rocking horse.

I knew when to admit defeat. As much as I wanted to find out what was going on with Charles, I never missed a deadline. I set down my handbag, shrugged off my coat, and resigned myself to the fact I wouldn't be leaving until my uncle was happy. I settled in, with Benji recognising the signs work was about to begin, and took up his usual place beside my desk.

"Let me see the changes," I said. "I'll have it done before we go to press. We can't have an angry vicar's wife speaking badly of you at the Sunday service."

My uncle patted my shoulder and handed me his scribbled notes before heading back into his office. I located the obituary in my tidy pile of files and made the adjustments.

I glanced at Bob, who hovered beside my desk. "Was there something you needed?"

"Just enjoying myself."

"Enjoy yourself elsewhere. You must have work to do."

"I never miss my deadlines. It's unprofessional."

I knew full well Bob regularly slid past his deadlines because my uncle would yank him into the office and yell at such a volume the entire newsroom could hear. But Bob was a capable journalist, so he clung to his job by his fingertips.

I ignored Bob's lurking, picked up the telephone, and dialled Inspector Templeton's direct number. The phone was answered not by him, but by an unfamiliar female voice. I asked to speak to him as a matter of urgency, but was informed he was working on a case. I left my name and reference about Florence Sterling's murder, impressing upon the woman he should return my call as soon as possible.

Bob was still lurking when I'd finished, and he was chuckling. "It's nice to see a pretty face like yours doesn't always get you everything you want."

"Regardless of whether my face is pretty or plain, I want to ensure justice is done." I checked the revisions I'd made on the obituary and added a few finishing touches.

"That nose of yours will get you in trouble one day."

It had gotten me into plenty of trouble already, but I wasn't interested in sharing my scandalous stories with Bob. "Isn't it time you headed to the pub? That's your second home, isn't it?"

"I'll be going soon. I'm waiting for the others to finish. I'd invite you, but it'll be men's talk. Your uncle is coming along. We're discussing my promotion."

I found that statement highly unlikely. "Good for him. Uncle Harry doesn't get out enough."

Bob stepped closer, but a warning growl from Benji persuaded him invading my personal space would be a foolish move, one that would result in a nipped ankle and a torn trouser leg.

Refusing to be intimidated by Bob, I swivelled in my seat and fixed him with a steely glare. "There's clearly something on your mind. Spit it out, or leave me alone."

"You're bad at this job. I completed a full-page spread on Florence Sterling in the same time it took you to botch together a couple of obituaries."

"I've written twenty obituaries in the last few days. At the rate people are dying, my uncle will need to hire someone else to write them, too. I'm more than capable of doing this job, and you know it."

He scowled at me. "You're interfering. You're doing more than writing obituaries. Everyone I interviewed about Florence said a nosy reporter had already been around asking questions that were nothing to do with her obituary. All you had to do was bung together a few flowery words in the death notice."

"Death notices and obituaries are different things. If you don't know that, you need to return to journalism school. Or didn't you go?"

His top lip curled. "I know you didn't."

I drew in a slow breath. "I learned my skills in other ways. On-the-job training is often the best way to learn."

"You're here because your uncle feels sorry for you. It's an embarrassment. This is a man's job."

As Bob berated me, he inched ever closer and was jabbing a finger in my face. I lifted my seat and stomped a chair leg firmly on his foot, then bounced up and down several times until something crunched.

He yelped and hopped back, howling in pain. Bob's foul glare would have withered a lesser woman, but I turned away and returned to my work.

"A female reporter will never get her name on a real story. If you're trying to steal my byline, Vale, you're in trouble. And you'll fail."

"Perhaps you should try poetry, since that rhymed." I'd heard this argument from Bob so many times that I barely registered his sniping.

"What's going on with you two?" My uncle strode out of his office. "Have you finished the obituary, Veronica?"

I handed him the revised paperwork. "All finished. Bob may need a couple of days off work. He's had an accident."

Bob limped to his desk. "I'm fine."

My uncle checked through the revisions and nodded. "Excellent work. That should keep the widow happy and off my back."

"Until the next time."

He grunted as he left with the copy in hand.

I worked on a few other projects, hoping Inspector Templeton would return my call, but by six o'clock, there was no word from him, and my stomach was growling so loudly that it was troubling Benji.

At a quarter past the hour, I pushed away from my desk. Inspector Templeton wasn't calling me back, which meant action was needed. I briefly considered going to the police station, but if he was avoiding me, it would be a waste of time, and it was in the opposite direction to my next port of call.

Other than one or two late-night reporters in the office, everyone else had left, so I bid them goodbye and headed into the chilly evening air. The London streets were bustling with people heading home from a hard day of work. There had been a minor altercation between two open-topped buses, and the drivers were studying the damage and debating with each other about who was to blame.

I was glad I had Ruby as my trusty, if somewhat speedy, chauffeur. I could handle a vehicle, but Ruby had experience few possessed. During the war, there was even an occasion when she'd driven a tank.

I diverted into my favourite little evening restaurant to grab a bite to eat. It was one of my preferred spots close to the newspaper because the owner allowed Benji to sneak under the table, and they always gave him a treat before we left.

Unfortunately, I was in such a hurry, I barely tasted the food and was soon back outside. To save time, I hailed a taxi and stepped out at my destination, Florence's former home in Belgravia, the address obtained from the directory.

I hadn't made an appointment to visit, so was happy to see the rooms bathed in light. Someone was home. I knocked, and a moment later, Kathleen opened the door. She looked ragged around the edges, suggesting she'd been hard at work all day.

"Miss Vale! Was I expecting you?" She dabbed the back of her hand against her cheek and attempted to tidy her hair.

"My apologies for stopping by unannounced, but Hank mentioned you were clearing Florence's personal effects from this address."

She nodded. "I've been here most of the day. Was there something you needed?"

"This is personal in nature. Perhaps I could come in, and we can talk?"

Kathleen looked concerned for a second. "Of course. Sorry, I'm forgetting my manners. I think I'm still in shock about everything that's going on." She stepped back to allow me and Benji inside.

"It's no surprise. Having worked with Florence for so many years, it'll take adjustment before you get used to not having her in your life."

Kathleen shut the door and led me into a messy sitting room. There were crates and boxes stacked around, many packed and looking ready to go.

"I've got a chap coming with a van tomorrow," Kathleen said by way of explanation. "There is so much here that I haven't been able to sort through it all. Hank told me to pack it, and he'll put it in storage. We'll have to deal with it another time."

"That sounds sensible. You don't need to rush these things. I expect you're attached to some of these items, just like Florence."

"Her tastes were fancier than mine, but she had an eye for beautiful things." Kathleen gestured to a seat, which I took. "Would you like tea?"

"No, thank you. It'll only be a bother for you."

Kathleen sat in the seat opposite me and settled her hands on her knees. "There was something you wanted to talk to me about?"

I drew in a breath. "There's no way of asking this question delicately, but did you know about Hank's affair?"

She blinked several times. "Before I answer, may I ask why you want to know? You won't print anything about it in Florence's obituary, will you?"

"No! I assure you, Hank is portrayed as a suitably grieving husband who lost a wonderful wife and had nothing but kind words to say about Florence."

"Why are you asking, then?"

"Because I don't think the police have the right man for Florence's murder."

Kathleen's hand fluttered against her chest. "Do you mean to say Hank could have been involved? That's why you want to know about his indiscretion?"

"I have my concerns about him. I visited him today, and I discovered he wasn't alone. He was with Eleanor Dixie."

Kathleen's gaze lowered, and she sighed. "I knew it would get out. They've been so indiscreet. It's not my place to say, but it was only a matter of time before people found out and the gossip spread."

"You knew about their affair?"

She nodded. "It's a disgrace. He is almost twice her age. I tried to look the other way, but Eleanor was always around. The second Florence left for work, she'd flirt outrageously with Hank. She was shameless."

"Hank was happy to reciprocate?"

"He seemed surprised at first, but he warmed to the idea. Oh ... I shouldn't say more."

"Hank was open when I spoke to him," I said. "It was an impossible topic to avoid since I found them together, and when I went into the house, it was clear what had been going on. He admitted to me his marriage to Florence was unconventional."

Kathleen gripped her hands together. "I didn't approve of that either. It seemed wrong, a married couple having dalliances with other people. But Florence was so free-spirited and passionate. She drew people to her, including me. I suppose when you're special, you have an abundance of love to give. That's what Florence told me, anyway."

I smiled tightly. "Oh, to be so fascinating and desirable."

Kathleen slid forward in her seat. "Florence must be remembered fondly. I would feel terrible if this news got out before her funeral. Or any time afterwards. She wasn't a bad person."

"The information won't come from me," I said. "But there is interest in Florence Sterling's life and death. You should brace yourself for the worst."

Kathleen huffed out a little breath. "The police are certain it was Charles. When they visited to tell me what was going on and asked me questions about him, there was no doubt they had their man."

"They've been to see you?" I asked.

"Just this afternoon. I've known Charles for years. He would write to Florence once a week, tell her his news and give his review of any performances he attended. She was his focus in life."

"Has Charles confessed to the police that he killed Florence?"

"They informed me they were only questioning him." She wiped away a tear. "It sounds as if they have enough evidence to charge him."

"What about Hank?"

Kathleen hesitated. "Hank isn't always to be relied upon. He drinks to excess and forgets things. I understand why you have reservations about him, but his affair wasn't out of the ordinary. He should have been more discreet and not entertained Eleanor's affections, but I don't think that gave him a reason to harm Florence. Eleanor was not his first mistress."

"Perhaps not." I sat back, surprised by the news about the police's intention to charge Charles so swiftly. It seemed too tidy, with so many other motives still in the mix. They must have something on him I didn't know about.

Kathleen stood from her seat. "I'm sorry to rush you, but I've got so much to do. Let's be thankful the police have their man, and Florence can rest in peace."

I nodded along as Kathleen showed me and Benji to the door. I said goodbye and stepped into the dark. If Hank had nothing to do with this murder, why had he concealed his entanglement with Eleanor from me? Florence was dead, so she couldn't object. Perhaps he was afraid of a public scandal.

There was still the unresolved puzzle of what the killer was looking for in Florence's dressing room. Did they know about her habit of hiding money and wanted it? That motive pointed to anyone close to her.

And then there was the eyewitness who saw Florence leave the Winter Garden Theatre and return to the Fireside Inn, but her body was discovered back at the theatre. Did Charles kill her and move her body? Or was it Hank? She'd have trusted him and wouldn't have hesitated to let him into her room.

Or was something else going on I'd yet to uncover?

I shook my head as I buttoned my coat and hurried away with Benji. There were too many questions in this mystery and not enough suitable answers.

Chapter 18

As usual, I ate breakfast perched on my mother's bed with Matthew on the other side, surrounded by a menagerie of animals. The kittens we cared for grew bigger and more playful every day, and Matthew had them in a basket on the bed. My mother's pugs were unsure what to make of these new additions and had had their noses batted and been hissed at several times for getting too close to the fluffy newcomers.

Ruby appeared in the bedroom doorway with a large brown paper bag in one hand and a sunny smile on her face. "Sorry I'm late. I took a walk to the beautiful bakery at the corner of Green Square. Every time I go past, I stop and stare at the confectionery. The owner is French. He came over during the war and set up shop. And I'm glad he did. I sampled a croissant on my way over, and it was divine." She pressed a kiss to my mother's cheek and smiled at Matthew.

"I'm unsure I like these fancy breakfast pastries," my mother said as she peered with delight into the bag Ruby set on the bed. "What's wrong with a plate of bacon and eggs?"

"Change is good." Ruby kicked off her heels and hopped onto the bed beside me.

"Change is stressful." Mother held a croissant in one hand and eyed it with suspicion.

"Try it with strawberry jam and a strong cup of tea. It'll be a taste sensation you'll never forget," Ruby said.

While Matthew and my mother inspected the croissants and debated over whether they were suitable breakfast food, Ruby leaned in close. "Have you figured out who did it yet?"

"Don't leave us out," my mother said sharply. "We know about the gruesome goings-on in regards to Florence Sterling. Such a tragedy. What's the latest news?"

"I know you love a good mystery." Ruby arched an eyebrow as she glanced at my mother's pile of paperbacks beside her bed. "From what Veronica told me on the telephone last night, the police may have gotten themselves into a muddle."

"A forgivable one, but a muddle we must rectify. Although I see why they're focused on Charles," I said. "By all accounts, he's not in his right mind. He had an entrenched obsession with Florence. He was at the Winter Garden Theatre the night she died, and he has no alibi."

"But he also claims he saw Florence leave the theatre and return to the Fireside Inn," Ruby said.

"He could be lying to confuse things," Matthew said.

"We also have Isabella, who saw Florence leave the theatre, and she saw Charles following her."

"Don't believe a word that woman tells you," Matthew said. "For all we know, she could be in on this, too."

I exchanged a glance with Ruby, then pressed on. "I have my worries about Florence's husband, Hank. He is overly fond of drink, and is having an affair with Eleanor Dixie."

My mother tutted. "Such a terrible thing. Who would cheat on a woman as wonderful as Florence Sterling? She was a pinup during the war. There were posters of her everywhere."

Ruby selected a croissant. "She kept the men's spirits up during the war. And we all admired her because she risked her life to perform for our soldiers."

"Hank could have grown tired of being a trophy husband," I said. "He was willing to talk about it, but it couldn't have been easy to know Florence married him because it made her star shine brighter. Because of her status, she caught herself a much younger man, and a handsome one to boot. Not many men would have put up with that situation for long."

"It doesn't matter how handsome they are if they can't stay faithful." My mother was already smothering her second croissant in jam, so it appeared the fancy breakfasts had gotten her seal of approval.

I reached over and grabbed one before the bag was empty. "When I spoke to Kathleen yesterday, she reluctantly admitted Florence and Hank had affairs, so maybe Hank's dalliance with Eleanor doesn't give him a motive. The fact he refused to admit they were involved to me is suspicious, though."

"There's still the money motive," Ruby said. "Hank married Florence hoping she'd turn up her toes before too many years had passed, but she was still going strong, so he got rid of her. As the husband, it's likely he'd inherit."

"When we first interviewed him, he told us he'll get something but not all of Florence's money," I said.

"With Florence dead, he's cut off a significant income stream." My mother dabbed jam off her chin.

I paused, the croissant halfway to my mouth. "That's true. He could have gotten desperate to break free and done something foolish. There are too many plausible motives. Too many suspects."

"You're having doubts about Hank being the killer?" Matthew asked. "Do you really think it was Charles?"

"What about the film producer?" my mother asked.

"Dirk Donovan," I said. "According to Charles, he was having an affair with Florence as well as planning to go into business with her. That's a messy entanglement to be in if things go wrong."

"And Florence was having doubts about the business arrangements," Ruby said.

"He was quick to protest his innocence when we met at the café," I said. "And he pointed the finger of blame at Charles."

"Sign of a guilty character," my mother said. "If you shout about something you didn't do, the chances are you did it."

"What about the ex-husband?" Matthew asked.

"I've checked his whereabouts," I said. "Clint is happily living a blissful retirement on Florence's hard-earned money in South Devon. And with Florence dead, he may find his retirement less easy going, so he has no motive for killing her."

"That leaves us with one more suspect," Ruby said. "Eleanor decided she'd been pinned under Florence's wing for too long and wanted to break free. Florence was stopping her from getting the acting roles she wanted, and she had the man Eleanor was interested in. Those are good motives for murder."

"I think it was Isabella," Matthew said.

"Isabella isn't even a suspect," I said. "She's after gossip."

"She was lurking in the shadows and desperate for a story. She'd do anything to get on the front page of that gossipy excuse for a newspaper she works for."

"I'm sure Isabella wouldn't stoop to murder," I said. "She is many things, but she's not that cold-hearted."

"She is! And I should know."

"Another croissant?" Ruby passed the bag to Matthew. "Sweet things cheer me up when I'm in a grump."

He took it, not looking any more cheerful, and sank his teeth into it, scattering crumbs on Mother's blankets, and receiving a scolding for his bad manners.

"Someone is lying to us," I said. "And we must find out why."

"Money, freedom, or revenge." Ruby ticked off the three options on her fingers. "Those are the most likely motives for this murder."

"Florence's killer was looking for something in her dressing room at the theatre," I said. "Something important enough to kill her for."

"And then we have the mystery of where exactly Florence was killed," Ruby said. "Isabella believes she died at the inn."

I nodded. "We must return to the Fireside Inn. Although, I doubt there's any evidence we overlooked. Reggie always gets the rooms cleaned between guests."

"We'll talk to locals and staff, see if there was anything suspicious going on the night Florence died," Ruby suggested.

"This isn't for you! You've already had two breakfasts." My mother held her half-eaten pastry above her head as the pugs attempted to steal a bite. "These are ridiculous creatures. Squashed faces, wrinkled skin, and teeth that aren't worth having."

"You adore them," I said, "even though I told you not to get attached."

"I'm not attached. They're off to the dogs' home soon. I would like to swap their collars before they go to make them look presentable, but they won't let me take them off. Whenever I try, they squirm away."

I checked the time. "If we're quick, we can go to the Fireside Inn before work."

"Veronica! Didn't you hear me?" My mother batted my arm like a high-spirited tabby. "Help me with the collars. We can't have the dogs looking shabby. Sarah is visiting later, so they need to look their best or she'll gossip with the other neighbours."

"Now? Is it such an emergency they have different collars?" I checked the pugs' collars. They were in perfect condition, although Quillon's had been recently re-stitched.

"Yes! Peregrine keeps scratching his neck, so his collar must be bothering him. They need to be changed, and with my swollen finger joints, I'm worse than useless."

I wasn't getting out of this bedroom until the dogs had been pampered. "I'll grab the box and see what I can find."

"It's tucked under the bed."

I was on my hands and knees when there was a knock at the front door. Ruby hurried away to see who was calling so early, and I was clambering up with the box of dog toys and collars when Inspector Templeton appeared in the bedroom doorway.

He nodded a greeting at everyone.

My mother patted down her hair and smiled sweetly. "Inspector! What a wonderful surprise."

"I apologise for the intrusion. I should have telephoned ahead before calling on you."

"You remember me, do you? I left several messages yesterday, and you didn't return a single one." I hoisted the box onto the bed and frowned at Inspector Templeton.

"Veronica, you're impossible to forget," he said.

My mother was ordering Matthew around in an attempt to get the bed clear of breakfast debris. "You're always welcome. And I must apologise for the mess. We don't usually eat like this. We always dine at the table."

Inspector Templeton's smile softened, and he turned his attention to my mother. He'd been by the house enough times to know exactly how we took our breakfast. "Please, there's no need to make an effort because I'm here. I won't stay long, but I know how eager Veronica is to learn about the investigation. And I was getting comments at work about the number of calls she'd made to me."

"I'll continue to make them until you return one." I inspected several dog toys in the box. "I've been nothing but helpful in this investigation, so the least I deserve is common courtesy."

"Helpful? Is that what you call it?"

"We've offered you suspects, alibis, and motives. And all we've gotten is ignored. That's hardly the behaviour of a gentleman."

"Veronica! I'm sure Inspector Templeton has been busy solving serious crimes," my mother said. "Please, take a seat. Matthew, remove those books from the chair so Inspector Templeton can sit."

He shook his head. "Really, there's no need to trouble yourself. I'll only be a minute."

Matthew shrugged, collected his basket of kittens, and ambled out of the room.

"Once Veronica and Ruby have the pertinent information, I'm sure they won't trouble the investigation any further. Isn't that right, ladies?" Inspector Templeton asked.

"Assuming you get the correct person and close the case in a satisfactory manner, you won't hear from either of us again." I grabbed a handful of dog collars and laid them on the bed.

"I should make you say that with your hand on a bible." Inspector Templeton patted Benji on the head. "Charles has confessed to Florence Sterling's murder."

I was so surprised I didn't speak and simply stared at him.

A faint smirk crossed Inspector Templeton's face. He must have been hoping for that reaction.

"Why would he do that?" Ruby asked. "He loved Florence."

"Charles also admitted to that. At one point during his interview, it was all he kept saying. His only interest was Florence. He'd follow her anywhere. He'd do anything for her. Charles's life had no meaning without Florence Sterling in it." Inspector Templeton shook his head. "His love was possessive, unnatural, and dark."

"Charles admitted he attacked Florence at the theatre?" I asked the second I had regained my composure.

"He admitted to watching her after everyone had left the party. He waited outside for her."

"And..."

"And nothing. We filled in the gaps."

"Did you search his lodgings?" I asked. "Find evidence of his intent to harm Florence?"

"We searched his lodgings."

"What did you discover?"

Inspector Templeton drew in a breath. "Nothing of note."

"Did Charles's landlady not confirm what he was doing the night of Florence's murder?"

"Mrs Beamish heard him come in. She wasn't happy about being disturbed." Inspector Templeton peered at the pugs. "Charles's landlady also admitted she heard him leave later that same evening."

"To return to the Winter Garden Theatre?" I asked.

"He admitted he went back."

"Did Charles also tell you he saw Florence leave the theatre very much alive and return to the Fireside Inn?"

"He did."

"And yet her body was found at the theatre," I said. "How did he explain that to you?"

"Charles is undergoing psychiatric tests," Inspector Templeton said. "We believe he has health issues. His instability caused him to attack Florence and then move her body."

"That sounds unsavoury to me," Ruby said.

"And outlandish," I said. "If it was Charles, what was he looking for?"

"He didn't say he was looking for anything," Inspector Templeton said.

"Someone was! Florence's dressing room was turned over for a reason. Did Charles steal something? If so, the evidence would be in his possession, yet you found nothing on his person or in his lodgings."

Inspector Templeton's nostrils flared. "We're tidying the loose ends. I thought you'd be pleased to know we had a confession. This is no longer your concern. Not that it ever was."

I fell silent and stared at nothing in particular. Something felt amiss, and I intended to find out what it was.

My mother tugged on my arm. "Veronica, this collar isn't suitable. It's far too heavy."

Absentmindedly, I took the collar she held out to me. It was heavier than it needed to be for a small pug, and there was a lump inside it. I turned it over and examined it. The seam had been cut and clumsily sewn together. There was something inside the collar.

"If you'll excuse me, I need to get to work," Inspector Templeton said.

"Tie up all those loose ends, I suppose," Ruby said tartly. "Charles never struck me as a violent man, just a lonely one. His affection for Florence was sweet, not sinister. Are you sure he did it?"

"I'm satisfied with our investigation," Inspector Templeton said. "If there's nothing else..."

I grabbed a pair of nail scissors from my mother's bedside table and sliced through the clumsy seam on the collar. I worked my fingers inside to widen the hole, turned over the dog collar, and squeezed out the lumps. Two large diamonds popped out.

Chapter 19

"They can't be real." My mother stared open-mouthed at the fat, glistening diamonds that sat on her bedsheets.

"Has anybody got a sharp knife?" Ruby asked. "It's almost impossible to scratch genuine diamonds."

"You would know that how?" Inspector Templeton loomed over the stones, forgetting all about keeping a respectful distance from my mother's bed. His behaviour was excusable, given the surprising find.

"A lady must know her precious gems so she can inspect her engagement ring to ensure it's of a suitable quality," Ruby said. "And if I had any of these giant diamonds offered to me on a ring, I'd jump on the proposer in a heartbeat."

"Why was Florence hiding her jewels inside her dogs' collars?" My mother shook her head. "The poor little creatures could have torn the seams open and swallowed them."

"Fortunately for the pugs, your daughter has an eagle eye." Inspector Templeton collected the diamonds in his handkerchief, folded it over carefully, and placed it into his pocket. "These could be evidence."

"What they are is the perfect motive for murder," I said. "And it now makes sense why Florence's dressing room was turned over. Someone wanted those diamonds."

"Clever Florence hid them in the last place anyone would look," Ruby said.

"These diamonds don't alter our investigation. They give us a clearer motive for murder." Inspector Templeton was already heading towards the door.

"You don't think Charles was after the diamonds, do you?" I hurried after him.

"He followed Florence everywhere. She could have done something with the collars and he saw her."

I didn't enjoy that theory, but it was possible. Charles had admitted to acting like Florence's shadow.

"Now we have these diamonds, we have everything we need to charge Charles," Inspector Templeton said.

"The pieces fit together in a certain manner." There was a note of caution in my voice. "But some of those pieces feel hammered home. You should question Florence's other friends, and Hank. I'm sure, with his extravagant lifestyle, those diamonds would have set him right for a long time."

"I'll see what Charles has to say first." Inspector Templeton pulled open the front door. "Please say goodbye to your family for me."

I watched him hurry away and climb into a smart black car.

Ruby appeared next to me. "That's it? The case is solved?"

I let out a gentle sigh. "According to Inspector Templeton. We should still visit the Fireside Inn. There's the mystery of how Florence was seen leaving the theatre alive and then her body being discovered there the next morning to be solved."

"Let's visit the inn now and see if Reggie can help with this puzzle."

Ten minutes later, and after several warnings from my mother about the dangerous damp and tuberculosis-inducing chill I'd suffer if I stepped outside, we were leaving the house at a smart trot. Benji was off his lead, content to run ahead of us.

"It's so cold, let's get a taxi to the theatre," Ruby said. "And I can't be late for work. Lady M is offering on the stallion we viewed. I'm so excited to add him to the stables. There'll be new foals before the end of the year if he proves his value."

"I'll have to visit when the foals are born. Let's give Benji ten minutes' walk, then we'll hail a taxi." I also needed a walk in the cold air to clear my head and get my thoughts in order. Inspector Templeton thought he'd solved this case. He had Charles in a cell and had discovered a reason for him to murder Florence.

Did this case really come down to obsession turned dark and greed?

"I feel deflated after the diamond discovery," Ruby said. "I should be happy. We now know why Florence was killed, but the victory feels hollow, somehow."

"It feels hollow because we're still missing something," I said. "Florence's pugs are at least ten years old. If she'd had them since they were pups, she could have been hiding her precious stones in those collars for almost a decade. Why did the killer strike now?"

"If it was Hank, Florence could have pushed him over the edge. He decided he no longer wanted to be married to her, but she refused to let him go."

"Florence has been married before, so she has no fear of the divorce court," I said. "And she'd have known she could land herself another husband when the position became available."

Ruby tilted her head from side to side. "Since the ex-husband's tucked down in Devon enjoying the high life, there'd be no reason for him to return to get his hands on the diamonds. And with Florence gone, his cosy retirement will have to become a touch more frugal."

"He has no motive. Kathleen would have known about the stones," I said. "Working as Florence's assistant, it would have been easy for her to remove the diamonds at any point during her employment, so she had no reason to kill Florence to get them."

"Florence could have caught Kathleen trying to remove them from the collars."

"If that happened, Kathleen would have been fired, or arrested." I shook my head, happy to talk through the options with Ruby.

"That leaves us with Dirk or Eleanor," Ruby said, looking around for a taxi as she briskly rubbed her hands together.

"Dirk could have become fearful their production deal was falling through. He was determined to get Florence's money, so he set his sights on the diamonds."

"What would he have done with them? I can't imagine it's easy to sell a stolen diamond."

"There's a taxi!" I lifted my hand to summon it. "If you know the right people, you can sell anything and get a decent price." I called Benji back, and we climbed into the taxi. I gave the cabbie the address for the Fireside Inn, and we were soon there.

It was early, so the front doors were bolted, but Reggie would be inside, sorting through stock to prepare for lunchtime opening. Sure enough, a quick tap on the door summoned him.

His smile was wide as he greeted us. "Come inside, you three. You must be freezing. It was brass monkeys out there when I came down. I thought I'd have to chip ice off the water before I could wash."

I chuckled. "I know full well the facilities are first rate and the plumbing is modern. My father oversaw those renovations."

Reggie's grin widened as he rubbed the back of his neck. "Just drumming up sympathy for having to be here not long past sunup for a delivery. What can I do for you fine ladies?"

"We need to see the room Florence Sterling was staying in again," I said.

"Of course. I don't know what good it'll do you, though. I had my cleaning lady in there after the police gave me the all clear." Reggie grabbed the key from behind the bar and led us up the stairs. He stopped by the door and unlocked it.

I stepped inside the clean, quiet room. It would have been impossible to tell that a few days ago, a superstar of the theatre and silent films had stayed here. Everything was neat and back in its place, the bed carefully made, and a faint smell of lemon polish in the air.

"Is there anything else I can do for you?" Reggie asked.

"Walk around the room with me. I'd like to know if there's anything out of place or unusual in here," I said.

He looked momentarily surprised. "Anything you like. What are you looking for?"

"I suppose I'll know it when I see it, or rather when I don't see it."

"Makes a curious kind of sense," Reggie said. "Where do you want to start?"

"Let's walk around the room clockwise. Start by the door and go to the dresser. Talk me through everything you see and let me know if it appears odd."

"Got it. I think." Reggie seemed uncertain as he started his tour of the room. While we walked, Ruby went in the opposite direction, and Benji put his nose to the floor and sniffed.

"Nothing strange so far," Reggie said. "The dressing table is in its usual place, and it's the same chair. The mirror is in good condition. You'll find a Bible in one of the dressing table drawers."

I opened the drawers in turn, and they were all empty apart from the aforementioned Bible.

Reggie stopped by the window that looked out onto the back alley. "The curtains look as they should. The cleaning lady didn't say there was anything in the way of dirt or dust on them." He walked to the next window, and we looked out. He stopped by the bedside table, which was clear apart from a small lamp with a pale pink shade. He tested it. "That works. And the bed looks normal. I'm not being much help, am I?"

"You're doing great, Reggie," I said. "I need to make sure the police have the right man for

Florence's murder. They're convinced they've got enough evidence to charge someone, but I'm uncertain. I must ensure we miss nothing."

Benji whined and lifted a paw.

"I'll get you some pork scratchings in a minute, boy," Reggie said. "The other side of the bed is the same. There should be nothing in the drawers. Miss Ruby, would you mind checking?"

Ruby looked inside the drawer and nodded. "It's empty."

Benji whined again. He hadn't moved from the spot he'd been sniffing.

I hurried over and joined him, crouching beside him. "Have you got something?"

He had his nose pressed to the floor and was staring hard. There was a dark, round splodge dried on the wood.

"Reggie, do you know what this is?" I pointed at the dried mark.

Reggie peered over my head. "Can't say I do. The boards get marked with age. That could have been here for a long time."

"Or it could be fresh."

"Huh! Well, that is odd." Reggie had backed away and was staring at the floor.

"What is it?" I asked.

"The rug is missing. Every bedroom has a rug. We put them down after guests complained about getting cold feet. The cleaner said nothing about removing the rug to be cleaned."

I stared at the bare floorboards. "There was no rug here the first time we looked in this room."

"It was definitely here before Florence checked in," Reggie said.

"Which means she did something to it, or she had a visitor who needed to make sure the rug vanished," Ruby said.

I looked at the dried mark on the wooden floorboard. "Someone attacked Florence here, and the rug became marked with her blood. Whoever attacked her needed to make sure there was no evidence in this room."

"They rolled the rug and hid it." Ruby dropped to her knees and peered under the bed. "It's not there."

"The police would have covered every inch of this room," I said. "It can't be in here."

"Not every inch, since they missed that stain on the wood," Reggie said. "Good boy, Benji. That definitely deserves pork scratchings."

"They could have assumed it was an old mark. They didn't have Benji's nose to tell them otherwise," I said. "If Inspector Templeton had let us all in the room the first time we visited, Benji would have found this straight away."

"Did anyone come up to this room that night?" Ruby asked Reggie.

"Not that I know of. Although, it's possible someone got in. As you know, guests have their own entrance at the back of the inn. It takes them into the alleyway."

I nodded. "It's for guests only? Not staff or customers using the bar?"

Reggie stared at the mark on the floor. "Florence liked to go out that way if there were any newspaper types lurking out the front. It's a discreet door that anyone can get in and out of without being seen."

"Can you hear the door opening and closing from the bar?" I asked.

Reggie's cheeks coloured under his dark scruff. "If it had been a quiet night, most likely. But..."

"Go on," I said. "What was happening that night?"

He looked at his shoes. "It was my card night. I had Mickey Flynn and a few of the boys over. We didn't cause trouble, and we were only playing for pennies. I didn't mean any harm by gambling on the premises."

"That's fine. You're in no trouble," I reassured him. "I'm only interested in knowing if Florence had unexpected visitors. Did anyone at the card game hear anything unusual?"

"They didn't say a word to me if they did," Reggie said. "They're a rowdy lot, so most likely drowned out anything odd. I'm sorry."

I reassured him with a brief arm pat. "None of this is your fault. Let's go to the alley and retrace Florence's steps."

Reggie locked the bedroom door, and we headed downstairs. He took us along the corridor to a door marked 'Guest Exit' and unlocked it. I stepped into a damp, slightly dingy alleyway. One direction would take me to the main road, and the other led to a dead end with a brick wall. There were sacks of rubbish piled up and several crates close to the wall.

"Be careful if you go that way," Reggie called after me as I headed towards the rubbish. "We get rats back here."

"You're looking for the rug?" Ruby asked as she followed close on my heel with Benji.

"This is the most logical place to hide it. Whoever moved the rug would have needed to dispose of it quickly. Someone would have noticed a person walking through the London streets with a bloody rug over their shoulder."

"You don't think that's how Florence was taken out, do you?" Ruby asked. "Wrapped in the rug?"

I shuddered. "I sincerely hope not."

Benji shot ahead, his nose in the air and his tail stiff. I followed with Ruby, and a few seconds later, we were peering behind a pile of crates. A rolled-up rug with a large dark stain on it was tucked out of sight.

"That's it!" Reggie stood behind Ruby. "I recognise the pattern."

"We'd better not touch it," I said. "The police will need to see this."

"Shall I telephone them?" Reggie asked.

"Yes. But before you do, Mickey Flynn, your gambling friend, he's the local pawnbroker, isn't he?"

Reggie's expression grew cautious. "You need to stay clear of him, Miss Vale. He's no good."

"Does he deal with stolen diamonds?"

Reggie's eyebrows shot up. "Err... Maybe. I stay out of his business dealings. I'm a respectable man these days."

"I know, Reggie. You're an angel," I said. "But I need you to arrange for me to meet with Mickey tonight."

Chapter 20

As much as I'd wanted to spend more time at the Fireside Inn, I never enjoyed being yelled at by my uncle for being late into work, and Reggie was more than capable of telephoning the police to let them know about the fresh evidence. After some reluctance, he had even agreed to set up a meeting between me and Mickey Flynn.

Mickey was one of the more amenable criminals in the area, who ran a somewhat respectable pawnbroker, while undertaking a number of shady practices best left unmentioned. If anyone knew how to deal with stolen diamonds, it would be him. I just had to figure out a way to get him to talk.

After a hasty goodbye to Ruby and a dash across London in a taxi, I'd barely settled at my desk before the telephone rang.

"Good morning, this is The London Times. Veronica Vale speaking."

"Veronica, it's Inspector Templeton."

"Goodness. That was fast. Have you been to the Fireside Inn already?"

"The inn? Why would I go there?"

I sighed. "You should check your messages more frequently. We found a vital clue there."

"A clue! I've just gotten out from interviewing Charles. I'm calling to let you know he wants to talk to you."

I was immediately on my feet. "I'll be there as soon as possible."

"Wait! Tell me about your discovery at the Fireside Inn. Does it provide more evidence Charles killed Florence?"

"Review your messages, and we can talk after I've spoken with Charles. Goodbye, Inspector." I set down the telephone, my heart racing. What did Charles need to speak to me about? Whatever it was, now wasn't the time to dally and ponder.

I grabbed my things and hurried to my uncle's office. "The prime suspect in Florence Sterling's murder wants to talk, but I must leave immediately, or I'll miss my opportunity."

My uncle had been looking over drafts of copy. He lifted his head and inspected me, then sighed. "Grab your notebook and get out of here. And don't come back until you've got me a scoop."

I grinned at him. "I won't let you down."

"Just be careful, that's all I ask. And there could be a decent byline in this for you if you pull off an exclusive for the newspaper."

"What's this?" Bob yelled from the other side of the office. "Women don't get bylines. Harry! I'm not having this."

I gestured for Benji to join me, and we raced away before Bob could poke his nose in where it wasn't wanted. Another swift taxi ride later, and I was entering the police station. The front desk was busy, and there were several people waiting to be seen. One poor fellow had a head wound and blood on his shirt.

As much as it displeased my manners to push to the front, I needed to see Charles as quickly as possible. I muttered my apologies as several people tutted and muttered under their breaths as I eased to the desk. "I'm here to see Inspector Jacob Templeton. It's about the Florence Sterling case. He's expecting me."

The desk clerk inspected his notepad and nodded. "Please wait by the door, miss. Someone will be with you in a few moments."

I waited impatiently, pacing with Benji. This mystery was so close to being solved. My instincts still told me Charles couldn't be involved, but I had to hear him out. If he'd done this, all my journalistic sensibilities would need to be thrown into the fire. Had I really gotten his character so dreadfully wrong?

The door opened, and Inspector Templeton appeared. "I didn't expect you so soon."

"A man's innocence hangs in the balance, so I came as soon as I could," I said.

"This way. Charles is in an interview room. We've been speaking to him ever since your diamond discovery." Inspector Templeton led me along the plain white corridor to a closed door. He turned to me before he opened it. "Veronica, I should warn you, you'll find a broken man in here."

"Broken by your intensive questioning? Didn't you tell me he was being assessed to determine his mental fitness? I hope you haven't been too rough on a vulnerable individual."

"Of course not! The psychiatrist's initial findings don't point to mental incapacity. And since he's confessed to destroying Florence's life, he'll be charged with her murder," Inspector Templeton said. "I'm only letting you speak to him because he won't sign a confession until you hear his final words. He keeps saying they have to go into Florence's obituary, and only you will understand."

I touched Inspector Templeton's arm, restraining my desire to burst through the door and winkle out the truth. "Thank you for giving Charles an opportunity to have his say. I'll report any pertinent information to you."

He arched an eyebrow. "You're not doing this on your own. I'm coming with you."

"Will Charles speak to me while you're breathing down his neck?"

Inspector Templeton huffed out a breath. "He knows the conditions of your visit. And behave yourself. You're a civilian, not an investigator."

I rested a hand on one hip. "Did you even check your telephone messages? There should have been one from Reggie, my landlord at the Fireside Inn."

"I know about the rug." Inspector Templeton's mouth thinned. "I've sent officers to investigate your discovery."

"It puts things in a different light, don't you think? And then there's the blood spot in Florence's room. Benji discovered that."

"He's a good boy." Inspector Templeton patted Benji. "But your findings change nothing. Charles was an obsessed fan, and he took that obsession too far. Florence fought back and shattered his dream, so he killed her. A bloody rug and a mark on the floor doesn't change the narrative."

I lifted my chin. Stubborn-headed man. "Let's speak to Charles."

Inspector Templeton pushed open the door and stepped in first. I followed with Benji and discovered Charles slumped in a seat. He appeared to have aged ten years overnight. His face was haggard, dark shadows sat beneath his eyes, and there were deep lines etched on either side of his mouth.

He pushed back his seat when he saw me, stood, and held out a hand. "You came! I hoped you would. I so wanted to talk to you. You haven't published Florence's obituary yet, have you?"

I went to take his hand, but Inspector Templeton cleared his throat and shook his head. "No physical contact."

I lowered my hand but gestured for Benji to comfort Charles. My wonderful dog headed to Charles, who had sunk back into his seat, and Benji rested his head on Charles's knee and looked up at him. I took a moment to compose myself and sat in a seat opposite. Inspector Templeton took the chair next to me.

"I heard you confessed," I said as gently as possible.

"I may as well be guilty," Charles said. "I care about nothing now Florence is gone. She was my life."

"You *may* as well be guilty?" I glanced at Inspector Templeton. "I thought you had confessed to her murder?"

"I as good as killed her."

"Let's have no more foolish talk," Inspector Templeton said. "You admitted you followed Florence the night of her murder. You knew where she was staying, and you even knew how to gain entry to the

Fireside Inn without anyone seeing you. You followed her from the Winter Garden Theatre and you attacked her. And new evidence has come to light that will be even more damning for you."

"What evidence?" Charles lifted his head, his red-rimmed eyes filled with curiosity.

"There's nothing damning about the evidence in regards to Charles's guilt," I said sharply. "But I found something on my last visit to the inn. Charles, do you believe you were important to Florence?"

"I hope I was." His gaze lifted over my head. "I loved her. Not in the way the police think, but I cherished her. She had to shine for the world to see, and that would never have happened if I'd been around."

I stared at him, and my eyes widened as comprehension hit. The words he'd used in his fan letters. The gentleness of his affection for Florence and desire to see her happy. His desperate longing to be in her life. His interest in her wasn't because he was a delusional fan. "You genuinely loved Florence, didn't you? You desperately wanted to be in her life, but if you had revealed yourself, Florence could have been ruined."

"What do you mean?" Inspector Templeton asked.

Charles nodded, and his gaze finally met mine. "Florence loved me in her own way. But I could never be a part of her life."

"Even though you deserved to be," I said. "You were her son, weren't you?"

Inspector Templeton shifted in his seat.

Charles nodded, his gaze drifting back to the floor. "I was given up when I was a newborn. When Florence had me, she was barely twenty and a rising theatre star. She was also an unmarried mother, and back then, a woman's reputation would have been torn apart by the scandal. I understand why she let me go."

"When did you find out you were her son?" Inspector Templeton asked.

"When I was eighteen. I was in a care home but adopted out to a nice family. I never felt like I fitted in, though, and I always wanted to know who I truly was. It took some digging, but I found the adoption papers in my parents belongings," Charles said. "Imagine my surprise when my birth mother's name was Florence Sterling. At first, I thought it must be another Florence Sterling, not the one everyone talked about. But the more I looked into it, the more everything lined up."

"What did you learn?" I asked.

"Florence went abroad for the last three months of her pregnancy. It was most likely arranged by an agent or a family member. When she came back, I was put on the adoption register, while Florence returned to being her incredible self."

"Did Florence admit to you she was your mother?" Inspector Templeton asked.

"I knew the truth, so she didn't have to acknowledge it." Charles thumped a hand on the table. "I just wanted her to say it once. To see me for who I really was. I had to know I mattered."

"Did you speak to her about this directly?" I asked.

"No, but I wrote to Florence just before she died and revealed everything. She knew me because I went to her performances, but she didn't reply to that letter when she found out I was her son." His sad sigh made my heart quiver in sympathy. "Maybe Florence didn't care about me."

Inspector Templeton sat forward in his seat. "While I appreciate you revealing this information, it only adds weight to the likelihood you killed her. You wanted to be acknowledged as Florence's son, and she refused you. In a fit of rage, you attacked her. You also wanted compensation for being abandoned, so you looked for her fortune."

"I care nothing about those diamonds," Charles said. "I never wanted Florence's money."

"You wanted her love," I said. "You wanted to be a part of her life."

"Yes! And if I'd wanted the diamonds in the dog collars, I'd have taken them years ago. I've known about them for a long time."

"How is that possible?" Inspector Templeton asked.

"I... I sometimes watched Florence through a window in her Mayfair house. She always forgot to pull the curtains at night."

Inspector Templeton let out a sigh, but I gestured for him to be quiet. We couldn't afford to have Charles go silent on us at this crucial juncture in the investigation.

"I didn't mean to pry into her private time, but no one was around, and I wanted to see what her normal life was like. I crouched outside the window and watched Florence put the diamonds inside the collars. She was terrible at sewing and stabbed her finger several times with a needle."

"Collars?" I jerked forward. "There is more than one collar containing diamonds?"

Charles nodded. "I saw her push diamonds into four collars. She could have done it with more for all I know."

I sat back in stunned surprise. My mother was sitting on a fortune.

"You really didn't want the diamonds?" Inspector Templeton asked.

"This was never about the money," I said.

"Exactly, but the police won't believe me. I'd never harm Florence." Charles reached for my hand but stopped himself. "I want that put in Florence's obituary. I need people to know I'm innocent and I was a part of her life for a good reason."

"We don't yet know you are innocent," Inspector Templeton said.

"I believe you are. And I will help," I said. "With your permission, the newspaper will print a story about you and Florence."

"Don't make promises you can't keep," Inspector Templeton muttered.

"I'll keep this one." I wasn't sure how, but I would get Charles a happy ending of sorts, and let the nation know about his connection to Florence Sterling. It would also be an opportunity to highlight the unjust treatment of unmarried women who found themselves in the family way.

"I don't want you lying about her," Charles said. "Florence ignored my letter, so perhaps she wasn't such a good person. She could have visited me. Even if it was to tell me she didn't want me in her life. I just needed to know she remembered me."

"Florence could have been taking her time, figuring out how to make you a part of her world," I said.

Charles rested a hand on Benji's head and let out a soft sigh of despair. "I should confess to killing her and end this part of my miserable life."

"Only confess if you truly are guilty," I said. "Otherwise, the killer will get away with it. You won't rest easy with that on your conscience."

"Veronica, do not attempt to change our suspect's mind," Inspector Templeton said.

I grasped one of Charles's hands and held it tight, ignoring Inspector Templeton's protests. "Charles, we know you followed Florence from the Winter Garden Theatre back to the Fireside Inn. Did you know about the guest entrance around the back of the inn?"

He nodded, looking startled by my grasp. "I sometimes walked along that alleyway. I liked to feel as if I was treading in Florence's footsteps. It made me feel closer to her."

"Did you see anyone else go in that way the night she was killed?"

"Stop putting ideas into his head!" Inspector Templeton stood. "This meeting is over."

"In a moment. Charles, what did you see?"

He stuttered then swallowed. "I told the police when I got here, but they wouldn't listen to me. They said I was making it up."

I shot a glare at Inspector Templeton. "This is important. What did you witness?"

Charles looked up at Inspector Templeton. "I saw Florence leave the inn. And she wasn't alone. That night, she had two sets of visitors."

"Did you see their faces? Do you know who they are?" I asked.

"A tall man and a slender woman arrived first. I didn't see their faces. They kept them well hidden. They were there for fifteen minutes, and then they left. They were in a hurry, too. I almost didn't have time to hide before they ran out of the alley."

My heart pulsed a beat of excitement. "Who was the other visitor?"

"We have no proof Florence received any visitors that night," Inspector Templeton said. "This could all be a lie to delay things."

"You have Charles's word, and I believe him," I said. "Go on, Charles."

"The other visitor was a woman. She wore a knee-length dress. Again, I couldn't see the face because it was dark. She also had a hat pulled down low. When she left the inn, she was helping Florence."

"How was she helping her?"

"I thought Florence must have had too much champagne because she was staggering. The woman had hold of her elbow and an arm around her waist."

"What did this woman do with Florence?"

"She pushed her into the back of the car she'd arrived in and drove off. That's the truth! I did follow Florence, and I did watch her. But that night, I wasn't the last person to see Florence alive." Charles's anxious gaze flicked from me to Inspector Templeton. "Do you believe me?"

"Are the police looking for these visitors?" I speared the inspector with a stern look.

"We've asked around. No one saw anyone coming and going from the back entrance of the Fireside Inn. I'm certain you've questioned Reggie about this same thing and gotten the exact same answers." Inspector Templeton gestured to the door.

"Miss Vale, do you think I killed Florence?" Charles asked. "All I wanted was to be acknowledged as her son. I wouldn't kill her because she denied me that."

I sat upright in my seat and held his hand even more tightly. "You're no killer, Charles. But you have been given a bad roll of the dice in life."

His eyes filled with tears, and his lower jaw wobbled. "I want to help. Please find out who did this to her."

I passed him a handkerchief from my handbag. "Thanks to everything you've just told me, we've almost figured out exactly who murdered Florence."

Chapter 21

Ruby took a brief sip of the dry martini Reggie had served her and shifted in her seat. "I'm all for treading the thin line between respectability and scandal, but are you sure this is a good idea?"

"We've dealt with shadier types than Mickey Flynn," I reassured her. My own martini sat untouched on the small round table. My stomach was churning as we waited for Mickey to arrive.

Reggie had been true to his word and arranged a meeting for us in the back room of the Fireside Inn for nine o'clock that same evening. It wasn't just Mickey who would join us. At least, I hoped it wouldn't if the urgent messages I despatched worked.

"Reggie was telling me about some of Mickey's more unpleasant behaviour," Ruby said.

"My father had dealings with Mickey, so he can't be that bad," I said. "Maybe the rough exterior hides a heart of gold. He'll do the right thing when he knows the diamonds are part of a murder investigation."

"Reggie told me Mickey's pawnbroker shop is a front for money-laundering. And that's not the worst of it."

"Reggie is trying to impress you with scandalous stories," I said. "He has a soft spot for you."

"He's a sweetheart, but he's not the right one for me," Ruby said.

"Not scoundrel enough?"

She gently snorted.

Benji's head lifted as footsteps approached the closed door. There was a light tap, and Reggie opened it. "Your guest is here."

"Thank you, Reggie." I raised my eyebrows at him, and he nodded. He knew to send through everyone else when they arrived and settle them in the adjoining room.

Mickey entered a few seconds later, patting Reggie on the arm as he passed him. He was approximately five feet ten inches in height, in a black suit with wide lapels, shiny black shoes, and a fedora hat with a purple band of fabric around it tilted at a jaunty angle. He was around my father's age if he'd still been alive, and had a salt and pepper scruff dusting his solid chin. He removed his hat when he saw us.

"Ladies, this makes a nice change, doing business with such pretty faces." Mickey's voice was East End London with a shaving of refinement.

"Please, take a seat, Mr Flynn," I said. "I don't know if you remember me."

"Of course. Although you were a youngster the last time our paths crossed. Who's your friend?"

"Ruby Smythe." Ruby introduced herself.

"Would you like me to stay?" Reggie asked.

"Everything is fine. Thank you," I said.

With some reluctance, Reggie closed the door. He had attempted to change my mind about meeting Mickey Flynn and discussing stolen diamonds, but Mickey was the go-to man in this part of London if you needed something illegal sold fast. If someone wanted to shift Florence's diamonds quickly, they'd have gone to Mickey.

Mickey dropped his hat onto the table, turned the chair around, and straddled it. He smiled at us, flashing a gold tooth.

"Would you like a martini?" Ruby asked. "Reggie has mixed a fresh batch."

"Don't mind if I do." He swiped Ruby's glass.

Her mouth thinned, but she didn't protest. Ruby was made of stern stuff, even though stealing her martini was one of the worst crimes a person could commit.

"Reggie said you had something that needed selling. Something valuable. Something that sparkles. What happened? Your fiancé leave you and you want getting shot of the ring?" Mickey asked.

I shook my head. "I'll come straight to the point, Mr Flynn. We need to know if anyone has approached you in the last few weeks about selling precious stones. Diamonds, in particular."

"Not selling, then. Looking to get yourself an engagement ring?" He downed Ruby's drink in one gulp.

"I'm capable of buying my own diamonds, should I desire them," Ruby said.

"Same here," I said.

Mickey's grin widened. "That I can imagine. Your old man always said you had a fire in your belly and you'd do great things. What are you doing with yourself these days?"

"Journalism. At the London Times," I replied.

"That's right! You have family in that business. An uncle, isn't it?"

"You're well-informed."

"It pays to be in the know in my business."

No one spoke, and we eyeballed each other. Mickey may be surface level friendly, but there was suspicion glinting in his dark eyes.

"Rest assured, I'm not here to break a news story or get you in any trouble," I said. "I'm sure you've heard about Florence Sterling's murder."

Mickey lowered his head briefly and placed a hand over his heart. "When I was younger, I once spent all day in the cinema watching her films. There was something about her. She had a way of lighting up the screen."

"She was a great woman," I said. "I'm writing her obituary."

Mickey nodded but said nothing.

I pressed on. "We believe the police have the wrong man in custody for her murder. We found new evidence, and it involves diamonds."

"Reggie said you have an example of the goods. I need to know what we're working with before I can say any more."

After Charles's revelation Florence had inserted diamonds into numerous dog collars, we'd dashed to my home and rifled through the box of toys and collars. We'd found a further three collars with diamonds in them, all of which I'd handed to Inspector Templeton. All except one, and that diamond sat in my pocket.

Mickey tensed when I reached into my pocket.

I arched an eyebrow. "You have nothing to fear from me."

"I've been around for long enough to know women are deadly creatures. All sweet smiles and laughter, but they're quick enough to slide a blade into your back when you let your guard down."

"It sounds as if a woman has done you a great wrong," Ruby said. "You need to find yourself a better class of lady friend."

Mickey chuckled. "Is that an offer, sweetheart?"

Ruby's cheeks flushed, but she kept her head lifted.

His laughter only grew. "I'm joshing with you. I've got to admit, I was curious when Reggie got in touch. Your father was good to me. He got me out of a few scrapes and even tipped me off when the Old Bill was heading my way and I had something hot in the shop."

My hand rested on the diamond. "I didn't know that."

"He knew when to keep his mouth shut. It was a shame what happened to him."

I accepted his comment with a nod and set the diamond on the table between us.

Mickey's gaze settled on the gem and he whistled. "That's a beauty."

"Has anyone been into your pawnbrokers asking about what to do with a diamond like this?" I asked.

"May I?" He gestured at the gem.

I nodded and sat back with Ruby as Mickey held the diamond close to his right eye and slowly rotated it. He pulled out a blade and scored the stone.

"This is legit. Even if it is stolen, I can get you a good price. Plenty of buyers on the continent who won't ask questions about its origins."

"We aren't selling it," I said. "But we believe the diamond will lead us to Florence's killer."

After another moment of inspection, Mickey set down the stone. "I had a customer asking about diamonds recently. She didn't give a name, and she didn't stay long, but I could tell she was nervous."

"A woman," Ruby said. "Young or old?"

"Average. The kind of woman you walk past on the street and don't even remember the colour of her hair."

"Not Eleanor." Ruby looked at me. "That means—"

Another knock on the door cut Ruby off. Reggie reappeared. "Everyone is here. They're in the room next door, just like you asked."

"Thank you, Reggie," I said. "Mickey, shall we?"

"Shall we what?" He remained straddling his seat. "I wasn't aware anyone else was involved in this. You looking to cut someone else in on this deal?"

"We haven't made a deal. And there's no need to panic, but I've brought together everyone involved in this investigation. Including the police."

Mickey's gaze narrowed to tiny slits. "I have no dealings with the coppers. They stay out of my hair, and I don't bother them. We have an ... arrangement."

"I'm sure that arrangement will remain in place. Your assistance will be looked upon favourably if you help to solve this murder."

His gaze went to the diamond. "Is there a reward for information?"

"There is," Ruby blurted out. "Given the high-profile nature of the victim, the police are keen on solving this and closing the case as soon as possible. You will be rewarded."

I didn't contradict Ruby, although she'd made a risky move, offering Mickey something we couldn't guarantee.

Mickey pulled a packet of cigarettes from his pocket, tapped one out, and lit it with a match. "I'm only doing this because I owed your old man a few favours. After this, we're even, got it?"

"Absolutely." I was curious about the favours they had exchanged.

He grunted his reply, then got up and held the door open for us. I was glad to see Reggie waiting outside. I could always rely on him.

We walked to the room next door, and I opened it to be confronted with Inspector Templeton and one of his sergeants, along with Hank Monroe, Eleanor Dixie, Dirk Donovan, and Kathleen Buchanan. None of them looked best pleased to be there.

Inspector Templeton strode over and caught hold of my elbow. "Your message said the killer had confessed. If it's not Charles, which one of them is it?"

"All in good time." I gently shook my elbow out of his grip and gestured for Ruby and Mickey to come in. Benji was already by my knee. "Thank you for coming, everyone. For those of you who don't know my companion, this is Mickey Flynn, a respectable business owner." As I talked, my gaze swept over the group to see who recognised Mickey. No one flinched.

"What's the meaning of this?" Dirk asked. "The message I received said if I showed up, I could settle my business dealings with Florence."

"And they will be settled," I said.

"Veronica, you shouldn't have done this," Inspector Templeton muttered. "Charles is willing to sign a confession."

"If he does, you'll have the wrong man," I said. "Charles Page did not kill Florence. But someone in this room did."

Eleanor gasped, her dark lashes fluttering against overly powdered cheeks. "What's going on? I thought this was about our film. Dirk, isn't that why we are here?"

He gestured her to be quiet.

I stood in front of the group. "The evidence initially pointed to Charles Page as Florence's killer. He's an obsessed fan. He followed Florence everywhere, and built his life around a fantasy of being in her world."

"We are all aware of Charles," Kathleen said. "It's not uncommon in this business. You get the obsessional types who won't leave the stars alone."

"I thought he'd confessed." Dirk looked at Inspector Templeton. "Don't you have the man in a cell?"

"We do. But new information has come to light about him," Inspector Templeton said.

"Charles wasn't following Florence because he was a devoted fan," I said. "He was following her because he was her son."

There was a group cry of surprise.

"Florence never had a child," Hank said. "I would know. She was my wife."

"She had Charles when she was young and had him adopted," I said. "She was an up-and-coming star, and having a baby out of wedlock would have ruined her. Charles learned who he was when he turned eighteen and he sought Florence out."

"Charles is a liar," Hank said. "Florence never wanted children. I approved. I've never seen the appeal myself."

Eleanor shot him a glare. "That's not what you told me."

Hank brushed away the comment with a wrist flick. "Charles is deceiving you in the hope you won't charge him with Florence's murder. And I insist you do."

I pulled the diamond from my pocket and held it out for everyone to see. There were a few gasps, then a stunned silence descended on the group.

"I can take that off your hands, whenever you're ready," Mickey stage-whispered close to my ear.

"Thank you, Mickey. I'll keep that in mind," I said. "Charles would have been charged with Florence's murder by now if it weren't for the discovery of this diamond."

"Is that Florence's diamond?" Hank asked. "If so, it belongs to me."

"Not so fast." I turned to Mickey. "Can you identify the woman who came into your shop asking about a particular product she wanted to sell?"

Mickey was glaring at Inspector Templeton, but his attention turned to the group. "That's the one. The dowdy one with the sensible shoes."

Kathleen's face grew ashen, and one hand was pressed against her stomach. "I'm leaving. I'm feeling unwell, and I still have work to complete."

Reggie was blocking the door, so no one was going anywhere.

I glanced at Mickey. He nodded. "It was her. I recognise the voice, even if I forgot the face."

"What were you doing at a pawnbroker?" Hank asked Kathleen. "I haven't authorised you to sell Florence's things, and I certainly wouldn't want you to sell her diamonds to a local crook."

"Watch it, fella. Unless you want to leave here with a few less teeth," Mickey growled out.

"I will have that diamond!" Hank gestured at Inspector Templeton. "Why aren't you arresting this criminal?"

"Because without Mickey's help, we'd have never known these diamonds were the reason Kathleen murdered Florence," I said.

Chapter 22

"No!" Kathleen's glare was defiant as she stared me down. "This was never about Florence's fortune. I cared nothing about her riches."

"You admit it?" Inspector Templeton asked, incredulity in his voice. "You murdered Florence?"

"I... I didn't mean to. It was an accident." She jabbed a finger at the diamond. "Keep that. I want nothing to do with it. Not anymore."

The group Kathleen stood with inched away, leaving her alone to fight this battle.

Inspector Templeton gestured at his sergeant, who moved to stand beside Kathleen. "We'll take it from here."

"You may need a few more pieces of the puzzle before you do anything rash," I said.

Inspector Templeton threw up a hand. "Veronica! This is getting ridiculous."

"You do want everyone involved in Florence's murder to be appropriately charged, don't you?"

He pinched the bridge of his nose, then gestured for me to continue.

"Thank you. Kathleen, you must have known about Florence's hidden diamonds."

Her bottom lip jutted out, and she nodded. "Florence didn't trust banks. She hid her money in all kinds of places. I was always finding bundles of notes and telling her to be more careful."

"And her diamonds?"

"I was aware Florence had a fortune in precious stones. She had relations with wealthy men, and they were generous with their gifts. I told her to put them in a bank vault, but she laughed and said she'd hidden them somewhere no one would ever find them."

"Florence picked a place she trusted over every other option," I said.

"Where has she been hiding those diamonds?" Hank asked. "I knew the old girl had some tucked away, but she'd never tell me where they were."

"Because you'd steal them and give them to one of your girlfriends?" Ruby asked.

Hank's cheeks coloured, and he cleared his throat. "The thought never entered my head."

"You promised me diamonds," Eleanor said. "I never saw any, though. I should never have trusted you."

"It would appear Florence was right not to trust any of you," I said. "In one way or another, you've all deceived her."

"I object to that accusation," Hank said. "I was a decent husband."

"Apart from carrying on behind Florence's back with her protégé, you were a perfect husband." I failed to hide the tartness in my tone.

"Florence would have understood." Hank tugged at his collar. "And what she didn't know didn't hurt her."

"Perhaps not," I said. "But I'm certain she wouldn't have been amused by your choice of companion."

Hank drew in a breath, then shrugged. "Perhaps Eleanor wasn't a sensible move, but she made her interest in me clear. I would never have suggested it if she didn't throw herself on me. I had a moment of weakness."

"You must have had many of those," Ruby muttered.

Eleanor turned on Hank and slapped him. "Rotter! This affair is over."

"I've done nothing wrong to Florence," Dirk said. "I've always encouraged her."

"Is that so?" I focused on Dirk. "You didn't visit Florence at the Fireside Inn on the night of her murder?"

"Absolutely not! I've already told the police what happened following the after show gathering."

"You were seen entering and leaving the Fireside Inn on the night Florence was killed," I said.

Dirk gulped and opened his mouth as if he wanted to say something, but then snapped it shut.

"We have an eyewitness who saw you and a slender young woman hurrying away from the Fireside Inn that night," I said. "I'm assuming you went there to discuss your failing business plan. Did you think you'd find Florence in a good mood following her performance and get her to change her mind about investing in your company?"

Dirk glanced at Eleanor, but she refused to meet his eye. "It wasn't my idea."

"Be quiet," Eleanor snapped. "There are no eyewitnesses. She's lying."

"There is a witness, and he's credible," I said. "You both visited Florence, but she wasn't interested in working with you anymore. So, you took matters into your own hands, didn't you, Dirk?"

"I didn't hit her!" Dirk said. "That wasn't me. I didn't lay a finger on Florence. I've already told you, I don't force myself on women. My reputation is clean."

I nodded. "I wasn't suggesting you struck Florence, but you forged her signature on the documents in her room, authorising her funds to be released to your production company. When we had lunch together, you revealed you used to be a method actor, and you'd immerse yourself into your characters. Unique clothing, a particular style of speech, even creating your own handwriting style. It would have been a simple task to get a copy of Florence's signature and practice until you were proficient. That's why you were convinced the documents in the Fireside Inn had been signed. You signed them."

"Is this true?" Inspector Templeton asked. "You forged Florence's signature to gain access to her funds?"

"I... I didn't hit her! That wasn't me. I never planned to go to the inn and harm Florence. I just wanted her to see sense. It was a golden opportunity, and she was passing it up because she didn't see a future in films. Her first love was the theatre. We couldn't go forward without her money. We needed her."

"Which leads us to Eleanor," I said. "Dirk, are you prepared to confess to the police that it was Eleanor who struck Florence?"

"Don't you dare!" Eleanor suckered Dirk with a vicious look, distorting her pretty face into a bitter mask.

"It wasn't me," Dirk said weakly. "I was loyal to Florence. I liked her. I just needed more time to get her to see sense."

"It was Eleanor who wasn't prepared to wait any longer," I said. "She felt overshadowed by Florence and stifled. She believed she no longer needed Florence's support."

"Look at me! I'm tiny. I wouldn't have the strength to hurt anyone." Eleanor's smile was forced as she looked around the group, seeking an ally, but all she received was suspicious looks.

"You always had a temper," Kathleen said, looking less ashen now the finger of blame had shifted from her.

"I only get angry when people do stupid things," Eleanor said.

"You considered Florence stupid because she wasn't prepared to recommend you for a starring role?" I asked.

Eleanor folded her arms over her chest and looked away.

"I told her we'd convince Florence to do the right thing," Dirk said. "I didn't know how desperate Eleanor was to get away from Florence."

"It was her own fault! She wouldn't stop talking at me, and she never listened." Eleanor sucked in a breath. "I never meant to hurt her. She grabbed me, and I pushed her. She hit her head on the corner of the dressing table and went quiet."

My heart stuttered at the confession. "Then what happened?"

"At first, I thought she was play acting, but I turned her over, and she was unconscious. I panicked. Florence had tried to get to the paperwork and tear it up, so I had to stop her. I... I never meant to kill her. I pushed her to slow her down, nothing else."

"Oh, Eleanor, how could you?" Hank whispered. "Florence looked after you."

"Don't play the innocent! She annoyed you, too. You were always complaining about her when you were wrapped in my arms."

Hank muttered something under his breath, a deep flush of shame crawling up his neck and onto his cheeks.

"Veronica, if Eleanor attacked Florence, then how is Kathleen guilty of murder?" Inspector Templeton asked.

"I'll get to that."

Mickey grinned. "Please, do. Although this is more fun than fleecing everyone at the card table."

"Neither Eleanor nor Dirk killed Florence, but they left her gravely injured and in desperate need of help," I said. "They must have hoped she wouldn't be discovered until the next morning, having bled out on the floor."

Eleanor and Dirk looked at each other. Dirk shrugged.

"So, it must have been a shock when Florence's body was discovered at the Winter Garden Theatre," I said.

Dirk stared at me with a questioning gaze. "I... I did wonder."

"You were also seen at the Fireside Inn that night," I said to Kathleen. "You helped Florence into a car and drove her to the theatre, didn't you?"

Kathleen's gaze flicked around the group. "I had to see her. I couldn't sleep, not since I found out Charles was her son. I went to the inn to reason with her. It was wrong that she abandoned her child all those years ago."

"How did you know Charles was her son?" Hank asked.

"Because Charles wrote to Florence just before she was murdered," I said. "Kathleen dealt with Florence's correspondence, and she read the letter. What happened when you showed it to Florence?"

Anger lit Kathleen's gaze. "She said Charles was her past, and she barely remembered him. It was a disgrace. I pleaded with her to open her heart to her only child, but she brushed me away. He was of no concern to her, and she wanted nothing to do with him. She even told me Charles was no longer welcome at her performances and to ensure she didn't see him again."

"Why did you care so much that Charles reunited with Florence?" I asked.

Kathleen's eyes clouded, and she looked away. "I was just like Florence. I met a young man, and we fell in love. I became pregnant, and he disappeared. He left me unmarried and alone."

"Why would that make you kill Florence?" Eleanor asked.

"I lost my baby, and the doctor said I would never be able to have another one." Tears trickled down Kathleen's cheeks. "Florence had the one thing I'd always wanted, and she ignored him. She treated Charles as if he wasn't a part of her. I got so angry."

"You confronted her at the Fireside Inn," I said. "Tried to get Florence to see sense and welcome her child back into her life."

"Exactly! But when I got to her room, I found Florence on the floor at the bottom of her bed with blood soaking her beautiful dress. I said I'd take her to get help, and I had a car outside. We got down the stairs, and I put Florence in the back of the car. I intended to take her to the hospital."

"But you didn't go to see a doctor or visit the hospital," I said. "You took her to the Winter Garden Theatre."

"Why not help Florence when she was so badly injured?" Inspector Templeton asked.

Kathleen's jaw wobbled. "Florence loved the wrong things! Even though her star was fading, she wouldn't let go. She refused to see everything she had. She could have had a wonderful retirement with people who loved her. Something not all of us will experience."

"You took Florence to the place most dear to her heart," I said. "You took her to the theatre to show her how unimportant it was and how it wouldn't save her."

"I decided Florence should die in the place she loved the most. If she was foolish enough to reject everything she could have, then she deserved death. Why should she live when she rejected the things that were most valuable?"

"You had to make sure Florence wouldn't survive, though," I said. "Which was why you hit her with a trophy from the shelf in her dressing room."

"She was dying anyway," Kathleen said. "I just helped her on her way."

Dirk snorted. "You're a monster. After everything she did for you."

"You're no better." Eleanor turned on him. "You despised Florence. When she wasn't around, you always mocked her and joked about leading her on and pretending you loved her. You only ever wanted her money."

He took a step back, startled by her vicious tone. "You were the one who shoved her over!"

"You both left her to die at the inn." Kathleen drew herself upright. "You're as guilty as me."

"I'm not," Dirk said. "I simply scrawled signatures on some paper."

"Which is fraud," Inspector Templeton said. "And you withheld evidence in a murder investigation. At the very least, you're an accomplice."

Dirk muttered a few unhappy words under his breath but made no further declarations of innocence. Not that they would have done him any good.

"Once you struck Florence with the award's trophy, what did you do with it?" Inspector Templeton asked Kathleen.

"You'll never find it. It's in the river," she said.

"We'll see about that. After you murdered Florence, you attempted to rob her?" he asked. "You wanted her diamonds?"

"I've already said I care nothing for them." Kathleen's gaze dipped. "Once Florence was dead, I realised I had nothing. I'd worked with her for such a long time that no one else would have me. I'm too old."

"So, while you were in her dressing room, you sought some of her hidden fortune," I said. "You turned the room over but came up empty-handed."

Kathleen glowered at the diamond I held. "Where did you find it?"

"In a box of toys and collars I took when I fostered Florence's dogs," I said.

Kathleen scowled. "I should have known those awful creatures would be involved. She trusted them more than anyone."

"You sneaky old bird." Mickey chuckled and rubbed his hands together. "When you came in my shop asking about selling precious stones, you must still have had your eye out for Florence's stash."

"I've heard enough," Inspector Templeton said. "Sergeant, arrest Kathleen for murder. I'll deal with Dirk and Eleanor." He turned to me and nodded.

I smiled at him. We'd solved the case.

Chapter 23

"Give them plenty of cuddles, short walks, time to adjust to their new home, and you'll have no problems." I handed Peregrine and Quillon's leads to Miss Smithson, their proud new owner.

"They are adorable. I've been looking for two angels to replace my wonderful boy. I lost him three months ago and have barely had the energy to get out of bed, I've been so heartbroken. When I called in at the dogs' home and heard two pugs needed rehoming, I had to see them. They are even more delightful than I imagined." Miss Smithson kneeled beside the dogs, treats already in her hand for their eager, damp little noses.

"They like to sleep in my bed." My mother had made a rare trip away from our home so she could vet Miss Smithson to ensure she was suitable to become the pugs' carer. "And I sometimes let them under the covers. I didn't want them to get cold at night."

"I slept with my boy on the bed, too." Miss Smithson smiled warmly at my mother. "I promise I'll take the very best care of them. They won't want for anything."

"I will miss them." My mother pulled a handkerchief out of her handbag. "Even though they were dreadful nuisances and plagued my allergies something terrible."

Miss Smithson stood. "I don't live far from here. You'd be welcome to visit. I'm home most of the time, looking after my elderly aunt. She's almost as excited about giving a home to these precious babies as me."

I nodded gratefully at her. Miss Smithson was a woman after my own heart. Sensible, no nonsense, and happy to support her family. And, of course, it was clear she adored dogs.

"My health doesn't allow visits outside of the house for long periods," my mother said with a touch of dramatic license. "The London smog is taxing on my lungs."

"Mother! We don't live in Victorian England anymore," I murmured.

She stared at the pugs, a flicker of hope in her eyes. "Perhaps a short visit once a month would be agreeable."

"We'd like that very much. My aunt rarely has visitors, so I'm certain she would enjoy your company." Miss Smithson bent to stroke the pugs. "The dogs' home has my address and telephone number, and I'd be most happy if they passed them on to you. We could have afternoon tea."

"I really shouldn't." My mother's gaze grew anxious at the thought of a social engagement she wouldn't have full control over.

"I'll be in touch to finalise the details." I gently took hold of Miss Smithson's elbow and guided her towards the door with the pugs. "My mother never likes to be a burden, but she will miss the dogs. Thank you for being so kind."

"Oh, no! Thank you! I'm delighted I could offer them a home. And after learning their owner died so tragically, I had to make sure the rest of their time would be filled with joy and love."

Although Miss Smithson didn't know exactly who the pugs' former owner was, she was aware her death had been sudden and unexpected.

"I can already tell they adore you," I said. "Thank you for supporting the dogs' home."

We said our goodbyes, and Miss Smithson practically skipped away with the little pugs trotting beside her, their short tails lifted.

"Am I too late?" Ruby rushed around the corner, her coat unbuttoned despite the chill in the early evening air. "Mrs M was a horror today. Nothing I did was right. She complained about everything, and she even made me rewrite a letter because she said my penmanship was sloppy. I've never been so insulted in my life."

"You made it. Inspector Templeton isn't here yet," I said. "We can't begin until he arrives."

"That's good. I want to look presentable for the photograph." Ruby greeted my mother with a kiss on the cheek. "Peregrine and Quillon have gone?"

"You just missed them," my mother said on a sigh. "I think they have a suitable new owner. But I have a mind to visit her regularly, to ensure the pugs are happy. Of course, that's if my health permits."

"You're as hearty as one of Mrs M's thoroughbred stallions," Ruby said as she tidied her hair in a small compact mirror. "You could walk from one end of this damp little island and back again if you had a mind to."

"Foolish girl. I feel so feeble that a gust of wind would push me over." My mother straightened in her wheelchair. "Veronica! There's your inspector friend. He gets more handsome every time I see him."

I looked out of the door again. Inspector Templeton strode towards us. Now Florence Sterling's murder had been solved, he must be able to sleep more soundly because he did appear refreshed.

It had been a week since Kathleen was uncovered as Florence's killer. After being taken to the police station, she'd confessed to everything. The discovery of the theatre door key concealed among her things had also helped to seal her fate, proving without doubt, she'd been there when Florence was killed. Dirk and Eleanor were also in serious trouble for attacking Florence at the Fireside Inn, leaving her for dead, and forging her signature to access her funds. It was the end of their film careers.

"Is that your friend from the newspaper?" my mother asked.

Ernie Brewster, a young chap with a pronounced limp who'd been hired by my uncle as an office dogsbody, was speeding towards the door with a large camera in his hands. He waved cheerily when he saw me and almost dropped the camera.

"Ernie's got an interest in photography, so Uncle Harry said he could take the photographs for this article," I said.

"It's nice to know some good has come out of such tragedy," my mother replied.

I nodded as Inspector Templeton and Ernie walked into the dogs' home together.

"It was a generous reward the police provided," Ruby said. "Although, after the hard work we did in solving the murder for them, it was deserved."

"Don't think I didn't hear that," Inspector Templeton grumbled as he arrived in the reception area.

I gave him a dour look. "You would have had Charles Page charged for a crime he didn't commit if we hadn't interceded."

Before we bickered, Ernie clapped his hands to get everyone's attention.

"Righty oh! Let's get everyone standing under the charity sign." Ernie's words always sounded as if he was wheezing for breath. He'd gotten caught in a gas attack during the war and suffered lung damage. He had good and bad days, but he rarely missed a moment of work.

"I need a word with Miss Vale before we begin." Inspector Templeton led me away from the group as they gathered to have their photograph taken.

"Don't tell me there's another reward for us to collect?" I asked. "If there is, the dogs will be thrilled."

"The reward money isn't payment for your investigative services," Inspector Templeton said. "You could have got yourself in serious trouble dealing with the likes of Mickey Flynn."

"Mickey was helpful," I said. "If it hadn't been for him identifying Kathleen and revealing she'd been asking about diamonds, we may never have uncovered what happened to Florence. I'm certain Kathleen was angry with Florence for rejecting Charles, but she'd had her eye on those diamonds for quite some time."

"Maybe so. You took a risk, you got lucky, and it paid off, but don't keep putting yourself into dangerous situations that are none of your concern."

"Your worry for my well-being is charming but unnecessary," I said. "I grew up around people like Mickey Flynn."

"No. Your father did. I've read his file, so I know what kind of business he was in."

I pulled myself upright and shook loose his hand, which had remained on my elbow in a most familiar fashion. "He may have had dealings with less respectable types, but he was a man of honour. He didn't break the law."

"Davey Vale broke it a few times, although never for anything serious," Inspector Templeton said. "What I mean is, you aren't your father, and you can only rely on his reputation for so long."

I smoothed my hands down the smart plum-coloured coat I'd worn for the photographs. It was always good to present the dogs' home professionally. "I don't like what you're implying. Even if my father hadn't known Mickey Flynn, I would have contacted him. I am not without courage, and I'm not afraid to step into dangerous territory to solve an issue."

Inspector Templeton drew in a deep breath and let it out slowly. "You should have kept me informed. I could have helped."

"What you would have done is exactly what you're doing now, and scolded me like I was a badly behaving child."

"You sometimes act like one."

"And you, sir, behave like you have a right to meddle in my affairs."

"I could say the same for you." He pinched the bridge of his nose. "I had my doubts about Charles's confession."

I snorted in a most unladylike fashion. "You had no idea he was Florence Sterling's abandoned child. And even if he had told you, I doubt you'd have believed him. You didn't listen to him when he told you about the comings and goings at the Fireside Inn on the night of Florence's death."

Inspector Templeton stared levelly at me. "This is a time we'll have to agree to disagree. We had a successful outcome. Charles has been released with no charge, and we have the right people for Florence's murder."

"The outcome is the most important thing," I said. "But next time—"

"There won't be a next time," Inspector Templeton said. "Veronica, I understand you may find civilian life dull. Your time in the war was—"

I cut him off just as rudely. "My time in the war is none of your concern. We both did our bit. I know you served, as did I. I also knew the conflict would end and we'd return to our normal lives. I have no issue with a sensible sort of life. But when a crisis occurs, I won't sit back and watch it happen."

"Neither will I."

I threw up my hands. "Then we are in agreement."

A tired smile crossed his face. "I don't know what I'm going to do with you."

"If you accept that I'm going nowhere, and I have a right to help others, we'll get along fine. What do you say, Inspector? Shall we call a truce? I find this bickering taxing." I held out my hand for him to shake.

He stared at it for a second, then gripped it tightly. "I'll be watching you, Veronica."

Inspector Templeton's warm hand held mine for an overfamiliar length of time, and a small shiver slid down my spine. "And I you, Jacob."

"Ladies and gentlemen, if I could have you all together for the photograph. Inspector, if you could stand in the middle, please. The ladies around you," Ernie said.

It was only then that I noticed everyone was watching my interaction with Inspector Templeton. My mother had the smuggest smile on her face. I tugged my hand away from him and turned away, an unwelcome flush of heat on my cheeks.

"Where are the volunteers with the dogs?" I asked. "We have plenty in need of adoption, and this is an excellent opportunity to showcase them to find their new families."

Molly, the centre's excellent receptionist, bustled out as if on cue, followed by four volunteers and eight dogs.

Ernie nodded and smiled. "Great idea. This should liven up the photographs."

There were several minutes of chaos as we arranged ourselves and got the dogs comfortable. I ended up with a fluffy Pekinese in my arms and Benji sitting on my feet. Ruby held an adorable three-legged white dog who kept licking her chin and making her squeal, and even Inspector Templeton held the lead of a handsome tan mutt with a waggy tail.

"Thank you so much for the generous donation." Molly stood beside me, cuddling a tiny black pup. "We were delighted to hear the reward money would come to the dogs' home. We desperately need to expand, but money is tight. People give what they can, but we know everyone is struggling."

"Veronica and Ruby were free to do what they wanted with their share of the reward," Inspector Templeton said. "I'm glad it's going to such a worthy cause."

We'd received our reward money yesterday, split with Mickey Flynn, since he'd provided a valuable service in apprehending Florence's killer. We'd spent a small amount on an afternoon tea in Knightsbridge, and I'd bought Benji a new collar, but the rest came to the dogs' home.

We stood for ten minutes having photographs taken, and I encouraged Ernie to get lots of extra pictures of the dogs. If I could sneak a few into the editorial and find these wonderful creatures the homes they deserved, it would make this task even more worthwhile.

Ernie finished taking the photographs, and volunteers took the dogs back to their pens for the evening.

"I should return to the station," Inspector Templeton said.

"We can't tempt you to adopt a dog?" Ruby asked. "The tan mutt you posed with liked you."

"It wouldn't be fair. My working hours are unpredictable, so he would be alone for a long time."

"Do you not have a lady friend who could care for him while you worked?" My mother's tone was innocent, but she did not fool me.

Inspector Templeton inclined his head. "There's no one I trust enough to care for any dog."

"That's a maybe, then." Ruby leaned over the reception counter and grabbed an adoption form. "You should leave your details."

"Let's not put pressure on Inspector Templeton," I said. "He's a busy man."

"You must come to us for dinner," my mother said. "Matthew would love to see you. And Veronica is always happy to have you visit."

I shot behind her wheelchair and pushed it to the door. "I'm sure Inspector Templeton has seen quite enough of me for a very long time."

"Dinner would be nice." Inspector Templeton followed behind us. "And I have been meaning to drop by and see how Matthew is doing."

"I worry about that boy." My mother gripped Inspector Templeton's hand as if he were her long-lost son arrived home after being at sea for a decade. "Your visits always make him smile. We're having steak and ale pie tonight. Does that not tempt you away from your paperwork?"

"It's one of my favourite meals. I'll be half an hour. Is that acceptable?"

"It is if you bring afters," Ruby said. "I meant to pick something up, but I had no time to even stop for a cup of tea this afternoon after being run ragged by Mrs M. I'm famished."

"I'll see what I can rustle up for pudding." Inspector Templeton looked at me. "If Veronica has no issue with an extra guest at the dining table."

"In the spirit of our truce, dinner tonight is acceptable."

"Yes, most acceptable." He nodded, and a trace of a smile crossed his face. He turned and walked away.

Ruby nudged me in the ribs with her elbow. "When you two stop fighting, you're adorable together."

"Have no fear. The fighting will start again before long." I watched Inspector Templeton stride away. If he wasn't so stubborn headed, he would be most pleasant to spend time with. "Ruby, would you mind taking my mother home? I can help you get her in a taxi."

"I'm not that feeble," my mother said. "Ruby can push me for a while, and we'll get a taxi the rest of the way. We'll need to keep watch for dangerous smog, though. If it gets in my lungs, I'm a goner."

Ruby looked at me with horror in her eyes. "Push the wheels in these heels!"

"It'll do you good, girl. Where are you going, Veronica?" my mother asked.

"I need to stop at the office. I'll be right behind you, though."

"Make sure you are. Inspector Templeton won't think much of you if you stand him up."

I stood in front of my mother's wheelchair and glared down at her. "To be clear, this is not a date with Inspector Templeton. You invited him to dinner, I didn't."

My mother chuckled. "We'll see about that. Off we go, Ruby. Tally ho!"

Ruby groaned as she pushed the wheelchair and headed towards the doors, which Ernie willingly opened for her, hurrying along beside her and asking if he could help.

I shook my head as I headed to the office in a taxi with Benji. My mother's attempts at matchmaking would end in failure. I had no head for romance, and my heart was most firmly closed to the idea.

I dashed into the office, quickly scanned the changes to the obituary I'd made, and headed into my uncle's office.

He was one of the few people still there, and he smiled when he saw me. "Did everything go off well with the dogs?"

"We got some wonderful photographs thanks to Ernie. I'll write up the piece tomorrow."

"Excellent work, Veronica. I can always count on you. Your name will be on the byline. A fun piece about a charity attached to you won't ruffle feathers."

I deposited the work on his desk. If my uncle had the freedom, he would give me more serious articles, but he couldn't due to the risk of a riot from my male counterparts. "If there's nothing else, I need to get home. Mother is expecting me. She's invited a guest for dinner. You're welcome to join us."

"Another time. I'm following a lead on a new story. Got some telephone calls to make. But before you go, you might be interested in this."

I was already at the door, but I turned back to face him. "A new obituary to write?"

My uncle nodded and rubbed his hands together. "A member of parliament has come a cropper. It's unlikely he'll make it. And he has a dog that needs looking after. Do you know anything about German shepherds?"

Inspiration

Although these books are fictional, I often find inspiration in real life. In Death at the Fireside Inn, you read about the Winter Garden Theatre and the Dogs' Home. Both have a long history and still exist today, although are very different places from their original forms.

The Winter Garden Theatre

This was a real theatre in London, its origins dating back to Elizabethan times (seventeenth century), and could be found on Drury Lane. It began life as a tavern, then was turned into a saloon, but transformed into a music hall in 1847, providing performances for 500 people. The music hall was re-built in 1872 and then again in 1891 as musical theatre grew in popularity.

The theatre closed in 1910, and the New Middlesex Theatre of Varieties opened in 1911. I used this theatre's exterior decoration as inspiration for the theatre in Death at the Fireside Inn. The exterior was red brick, Portland stone, and granite.

Inside the theatre were almost 2,000 seats and room for another 1,000 who could stand to watch the shows.

Although originally the focus was on musical theatre, as films gained in popularity, they were shown from 1912.

The theatre had another makeover into a flamboyant French style, which was my inspiration for the interior of the fictional theatre, and re-opened as the Winter Garden Theatre in 1919 with *Kissing Time*, a musical play by Guy Bolton and P.G. Woodhouse, which ran for 430 performances!

The times continued to change, and the theatre was taken over by the Rank Organisation in 1945, but the doors closed in 1960, when the theatre was under-used. Sadly, the beautiful building was left to decay before being pulled down in 1965.

A new theatre has since been built and has changed hands and names several times. Its latest incarnation is the Gillian Lynne Theatre, named in 2018 and owned by Andrew Lloyd Webber.

The Dogs' Home

This wonderful charity is better known as Battersea Cats and Dogs' Home in London. Back when it was founded in 1860, it was called the Temporary Home for Lost and Starving Dogs.

Started by Mary Tealby, she offered a temporary place for owners who lost their dogs. Her work helping lost and stray dogs was continued after her death by her brother, Reverend Edward Bates, who established a group to support the charitable activities, with support from wealthy patrons. At one point, they were taking in almost 900 dogs a month.

As the work grew, so did the complaints. 900 dogs barking would test the most stalwart animal lover! This prompted a move to the charity's current base in 1871 to Battersea Park Road in London.

The charity grew from its humble origins and now spends over £37,000 a day on helping lost and stray animals and finding them new homes. Many of you will have seen the wonderful TV programme, *For the Love of Dogs*, which was filmed at Battersea, and shows how far the charity has come.

There was also a fascinating series of photographs and drawings released by Battersea to mark their 160th anniversary and featured in the British newspaper the Daily Mail.

You can find them here:

https://www.dailymail.co.uk/femail/article-8872783/ Battersea-Dogs-Cats-Home-releases-photographic-hi story.html

Also By

Death at the Fireside Inn
Death at the Drunken Duck

More mysteries coming soon. While you wait, why not
investigate the back catalogue of K.E. O'Connor (Kitty's
alter ego.)

About the Author

Immerse yourself into Kitty Kildare's cleverly woven historical British mysteries. Follow the mystery in the Veronica Vale Investigates series and enjoy the dazzle and delights of 1920s England. Kitty is a not-so-secret pen name of established cozy mystery author K.E. O'Connor, who decided she wanted to time travel rather than cast spells! Enjoy the twists and turns.

Join in the fun and get Kitty's newsletter (and secret wartime files about our sleuthing ladies!)

Newsletter: https://BookHip.com/JJPKDLB
Website: www.kittykildare.com
Facebook: www.facebook.com/kittykildare

Printed in Great Britain
by Amazon